BAYOU
HEAT

ALEXANDRA IVY

LAURA WRIGHT

ANGEL

ALEXANDRA IVY

CHAPTER 1

An electric buzz raced through the New Orleans hospital. The sort of buzz that could only mean one thing…

Dr. Angel Savary had just arrived.

With muffled giggles, the female staff scrambled to catch sight of the tall man, whose lean body was currently emphasized by a light cashmere sweater and black jeans. Not that the women gave a shit what he was wearing. All of them, even the elderly charge nurse, fantasized about tearing off his clothes to expose the chiseled muscles they could see rippling with every fluid movement.

Yum.

And if his lickable body wasn't enough, he was also flat-out gorgeous. His hair was white-gold and clipped short while his eyes were as dark as polished ebony. A startling contrast that never failed to capture attention.

And his features…they were stunningly beautiful.

Not effeminate.

There was no doubt he was all male. Raw, dangerous, lethally sexy male.

But his features were finely chiseled and

gorgeous enough to melt a woman's heart, not to mention her panties.

Today, there was an extra buzz in the air as another man strolled down the corridor at Angel's side. No one recognized the six-foot-plus male with golden hair and gold-green eyes, but he made more than one female sigh with pleasure.

Ignoring the avid gazes that followed him as he strolled down the hallway, Angel led his companion into his office and firmly shut the door.

Instantly he grimaced. The large room that was elegantly furnished with a heavy walnut desk and matching bookshelves had always seemed comfortable enough. Especially since he spent only a few days a month at the hospital, preferring to remain in the Wildlands as much as possible. Now he realized the space hadn't been designed to accommodate two alpha puma shifters.

Leaning against the edge of his desk, Angel leashed his cat's aggressive reaction to the prickles of heat that filled the air. Not easy when Raphael, the leader of the Suits, was prowling from one end of the office to the other.

"Have you found anything?" the older male demanded.

Angel's lips twitched. Raphael was a skilled Diplomat, but the past few months had taken their toll on all of them.

A crazed goddess. The near extinction of their species. A traitor. And now a new enemy was creeping out of the shadows, threatening to be equally dangerous to the Pantera.

They were all twitchy.

"It's only been two days," he reminded his companion.

Raphael came to a halt, folding his arms over his chest as he studied Angel with a lift of his brows.

"Like I said. Did you find anything?"

"Pushy bastard," Angel muttered. He'd returned to New Orleans after it was discovered that human women were being impregnated with Pantera semen. The medical community wasn't that large. There had to be someone who knew something. Unfortunately, the laws regarding patient privacy meant that it'd been more difficult than he'd anticipated. "My searches haven't produced any direct connection to the Haymore Center," he at last admitted.

"But?" Raphael prompted.

"I traced a series of blood samples and reports being sent to labs in both New York and Miami."

"Is that unusual?"

Angel lifted his hand to rub the tense muscles at the back of his neck. Damn. He couldn't remember the last time he'd slept more than an hour or two. They'd been in constant crisis mode for so long it was becoming the new normal.

"There's a rigid protocol that the hospital uses to protect their patients' privacy."

Raphael scowled. "Explain."

Angel reached behind him to pick up a stack of papers from his desk. He'd gone through them a dozen times over the past forty-eight hours.

"They have specific codes in the computer system," he explained, pointing toward the rows of

3

numbers that lined the left side of the papers. "They use well-known, highly respected laboratories." He shuffled through the papers to the delivery forms at the bottom of the stack. "And if they transport specimens they use the same courier service each time."

Raphael gave a nod. "And the ones you traced?"

Angel replaced the papers on the desk, his expression grim. He'd nearly missed the orders for blood work, as well as DNA testing on a handful of patients. It was only because he'd specifically been looking for anything the least bit sketchy that he'd spotted the odd requests.

"They were listed in the computer with encrypted codes," he said. He hadn't actually printed off any of the paperwork, afraid it would alert whoever was going to such an effort to keep them secret. "They were sent to labs that aren't listed in any directory and the samples were transported by a private company."

"There could be a legitimate explanation—" Raphael shook his head, realizing what he'd just said. No hospital would go against policies and procedures. Not in this age of malpractice lawsuits. "Okay, it's probably illegitimate, but it might not have anything to do with us," he added.

Angel shrugged. He couldn't argue. It didn't matter how hard a hospital tried. It was impossible to avoid human nature. Creative accounting. Prescription fraud... "It's all I got for now."

Raphael resumed his pacing. Larger than Angel, the male was wearing a pair of black silk pants and white shirt that he chose in an effort to look more civilized.

"Was there a pattern?" the older male at last asked.

"Women of childbearing years. And infants."

Raphael sucked in a sharp breath, fully understanding why Angel had been so interested.

They didn't understand exactly what the Haymore Center had been trying to accomplish before Stanton Locke had burned it to the ground, but it certainly involved Pantera, pregnant human women, and babies.

"Shit."

Angel gave a sharp laugh. "Trust you to sum it up in one word," he drawled. "No wonder you're a Diplomat."

Raphael flipped him off. The two had been friends for decades despite the fact they were both alphas. They'd been drawn together by their mutual devotion to their people and their willingness to sacrifice whatever necessary to protect the Wildlands.

"Any clue who might be responsible?"

"It has to be an administrator at the hospital," Angel readily answered. He'd devoted hours to deciding who could be secretly testing the patients. "Only someone with a high security clearance would have the clearance to access every step of the procedure without alerting someone along the way."

Raphael cocked his brow. "That narrows the process."

Angel nodded. It did.

"There are five I intend to investigate further."

Raphael glanced toward the desk that was stacked with files. Angel had taken a temporary leave from accepting new patients, but there was a constant flood of paperwork. Sometimes he suspected humans made shit up that he was supposed to fill out just to piss him off.

"Do you need Xavier?"

"No." Angel wasn't a computer whiz, but he had enough training that he could run the necessary searches. "It's better if I try to do this internally. Besides, Xavier has enough to do with tracking down Hiss." He studied Raphael's grim expression, noticing the lines of stress etched on his friend's bronzed face. No one took the disappearance of the traitorous Pantera any harder than Raphael. Wait. Maybe Parish, the leader of the Hunters. That male had nearly lost his fucking mind when it was revealed that someone had managed to slip past their guards and take the male who had betrayed them. "Any luck?"

"Nothing so far," Raphael admitted, his voice thick with frustration. "Payton is working with Lydia to track and sort through Locke's finances to locate any other properties where Hiss might be hidden." Angel nodded. Stanton Locke was the human who owned the Haymore Center. They all hoped that by finding the man, they could not only locate Hiss, but the bastard would reveal his nefarious plans toward the Pantera. "And the Healers are trying to work with both Reny and Séverin to try and recover their lost memories."

Both the Pantera had been held in secret labs, although both struggled to recall precisely what'd happened during their captivity.

There was the potent stench of perfume before the

6

door was shoved open to reveal a tall woman with bleached blond hair and a lush figure.

"Dr. Savary."

Sashaying into the office, the woman came to an abrupt halt as she caught sight of Raphael standing in the center of the room. Her eyes widened, a blush stealing to her cheeks before she sought out Angel's amused gaze. The woman didn't know she was in the room with two puma shifters, but her body was reacting to their potent pheromones.

"Hello, Elan," he murmured in a low voice that made her visibly shiver.

"Forgive me, I thought you were alone."

He offered a regretful smile. "Perhaps we can speak later?"

"Yes," she breathed, obediently backing out of the office. "Of course."

Waiting until the door closed behind her retreating form, Raphael sent him a mocking glance.

"No wonder you don't mind working overtime."

Angel shook his head. The woman was beautiful. And she'd made it painfully clear she was available. But she was nothing more than a tool.

"Elan happens to be the personal assistant to the Director of Finance for the hospital," he said. "She has the codes I need to get into the man's computer."

Raphael heaved a deep sigh. "Damn."

"What?"

"I hoped you'd decided there was more to life than duty."

Angel gave a snort. Like any cat, he loved to play. And there'd been more than a few females who'd warmed his bed over the years. But from the day he'd watched his mother die from a rare Pantera disease, he'd focused all his energies on his work as a Healer.

He hadn't been able to save his mother, but he could save others.

"Isn't that the pot calling the kettle black, or some such shit?" he demanded.

Raphael shrugged. "I might have been a little obsessed with my responsibilities."

Angel folded his arms over his chest. "A little?"

The older male's lips twitched. "But I managed to have enough fun to end up with a gorgeous mate and a precious daughter."

"Which is exactly why I prefer to concentrate on duty," Angel drawled.

He was happy as hell for his friend. The male was clearly besotted with his mate and daughter. But Angel had no intention of ever committing himself to another.

"It happens to the best of us," Raphael assured him.

Angel waved aside the warning. "It clearly *hasn't* happened to the best of us and if I have any say in the matter, it never will."

Raphael chuckled, an unbearably smug expression on his face. "Luckily you don't have a say. Fate is a ruthless bitch who will bite you in the ass every time."

Angel ignored the tiny shiver of premonition that inched down his spine.

Nope. It wasn't going to happen. His duty as a Healer was all that mattered.

"Is there anything else?" he asked.

Raphael stepped forward to grab his shoulder. "Be careful, *mon ami*."

"I'm not a Geek, but I have enough skill to keep my investigations from being discovered."

Raphael's fingers tightened on his shoulder. "I don't question your abilities, Angel, but this new enemy has training, discipline and contacts in high places," Raphael said, his eyes smoldering with a fierce frustration. They'd all hoped that life would return to a simple existence once the goddess Shakpi had reunited with her sister. Now they were forced to accept that peace was still nothing more than a distant dream. "Worse, we have no idea what their endgame is. We're all in danger."

"I have no intention of taking unnecessary risks," Angel promised his friend. "No one in the hospital suspects I'm anything but Dr. Savary."

Raphael grimaced. "That's what we hope."

"What do you mean?"

"We have no idea what Hiss might have revealed."

Angel flinched. It didn't matter how many times he reminded himself the male Pantera was a traitor, it didn't get any easier to accept.

"I know that Hiss was a part of the disciples who were helping Shakpi, but you don't think he's working with this new enemy, do you?"

Raphael's face hardened to a bleak mask. "I'm not going to make the mistake of taking anything for granted." He shook his head. "Not again."

"Understandable, but Hiss seemed as baffled as

the rest of us when the bastards revealed they were willing to trade Rosalie and Mercier to get their hands on him," Angel reminded his friend.

Angel had been in the Wildlands clinic when they'd brought in Hiss, and while the traitor had refused to speak to anyone but the elders, he'd genuinely appeared confused by the fact the newest enemy had been so anxious to get their hands on him.

"He could have been faking his response," Raphael pointed out. "He's proven he can live a lie for years."

"I suppose," Angel muttered, not convinced.

Raphael shrugged. "Or he might have been unaware of them and now has decided they're his best shot at destroying us."

Angel gave a grudging nod. There was so much hate inside Hiss it was impossible to guess what he might do.

Still…

"I hoped he could be redeemed," he muttered.

"We all hoped." Raphael gave his shoulder a squeeze before he dropped his hand and stepped back. "For now, however, we have to be realistic. The bastard betrayed us once. There's no reason he wouldn't betray us again."

Painfully true.

"Shit," Angel growled.

***

The elementary school had been shabby before hurricane Katrina had slammed into the red brick

10

building, leaving behind utter destruction. On the plus side, the outer structure was reasonably intact, the electricity and water still worked, and a large playground kept it isolated from the rest of the neighborhood. Which meant no one came around poking their noses into things that were none of their business.

Indy had located the place when they'd first arrived in New Orleans from New York six months ago. At the time she'd hoped they would be in and out of town in less than a week. Which meant the need for secrecy had outweighed the desire for comfort.

Now she was glad she'd found a place where she could hold a prisoner without attracting unwanted attention.

Pausing in front of a mirror in the bathroom, Indy brushed her teeth and ran a comb through the short strands of her midnight black hair. She even took time to make sure there was no dirt marring her thin, pale face that was dominated by a pair of dark blue eyes and a mouth that always seemed too large for her face. One of the few men she'd briefly dated had called it 'lush.'

She grimaced. Although she was a grown-ass woman, she appeared to be in her early teens. An image that was only reinforced by the fact she barely topped five foot two and had a boyish frame.

Pulling a leather coat over her white muscle shirt that was tucked into a pair of faded jeans, she shoved her feet into a pair of motorcycle boots and headed out.

So, she looked like a biker pixie doll.

It was better than being mistaken for a pubescent boy.

She walked down the hallway that was filled with broken lockers and assorted rubble, entering the room that used to be the nurse's office.

Instantly a woman with long red hair and light brown eyes turned from the narrow bed, her face still beautiful although she looked older than her thirty years.

"How is she?" Indy demanded, remaining beside the door as her gaze slid to the tiny girl lying motionless on the bed.

Karen bit her lower lip. "Willa is a fighter, but…"

Indy's heart clenched with pain as Karen's voice drifted away.

"She's fading," Indy spoke the words that everyone was thinking.

Karen gave a slow nod, her eyes filling with tears. "Yes."

Indy squared her shoulders, her decision made. "I can't wait any longer."

With a glance toward the sleeping child, Karen crossed the cracked linoleum floor to stand directly in front of her.

"Indy, it's too dangerous," she whispered in urgent tones.

Indy shrugged. She'd been doing things that were too dangerous for the past ten years. Okay, she'd never tried to kidnap a full-grown Pantera male before. But she'd risked her neck a dozen times sneaking into the labs of her enemy and releasing captives.

How much harder could this be?

Unwilling to actually consider the question, or the odd flutter of excitement, she nodded her head toward the bed.

"What choice do we have?" she demanded. "The human doctors haven't been able to help Willa. We have to hope a Pantera can do better."

It'd felt like fate when she'd left the hospital yesterday afternoon. At the time she'd been frantic with worry as she'd carried Willa away from yet another doctor who'd been unable to explain the girl's debilitating headaches and fever that would come and go without warning.

But then she'd caught the unmistakable scent of Pantera.

Sending Willa back to the abandoned school with Tarin, one of the young men she'd rescued over the years, she'd trailed behind the tall stranger with white-gold hair until he'd disappeared into a private office.

Dr. Savary.

She knew then he had to be one of the mysterious healers she'd heard whispered about in the lab when she was still a captive.

Perhaps the one person in the entire world capable of helping Willa.

Karen studied her determined expression with blatant concern.

"If you bring the male here you expose us all to the beast-men."

Indy reached to grab her friend's hand. She thrived on danger, but she wasn't the only one who might be hurt by the arrival of a Pantera.

The beast-men might have been kept strictly

separated from the humans in the labs, but Indy knew enough about the creatures to realize that they were ruthless predators who would kill without mercy.

"It's a risk, and if anyone prefers to bail, I completely understand," she said.

She meant every word. Over the years she'd rescued over twenty captives from Benson Enterprises and the various annexes. Some had returned to their families. Some had simply disappeared. But five had remained with her, moving from place to place as she'd avoided the hired thugs who were constantly searching for her. The last thing she wanted was to put them in even more danger.

Karen scowled at her perfectly reasonable explanation.

"Don't be an idiot. No one is going to bail," the woman assured her. "We all love Willa as much as you."

"Yes," Indy agreed with a small sigh. They did. In less than six months the little girl had stolen all their hearts.

"And just as importantly we all know what we owe you," Karen continued.

Indy scowled. "Don't say that. No one owes me a damned thing."

"You saved us."

Tugging her hand free, Indy shrugged aside the woman's soft words.

"I was screwing with the guards," she muttered. She hated when Karen got all mushy. "Nothing pisses them off more than losing a prisoner."

"So tough." Karen gave a resigned shake of her

head. "Why can't you just admit that you're one of the good guys?"

Indy snorted. Who wanted to be a good guy? They always finished last.

"I'm a thief, a liar, and I'm about to become a kidnapper," she pointed out in dry tones. "Hardly the stuff of heroes."

Karen's pretty face softened with genuine affection. "Say what you want, Indy. You have our loyalty. We'll stand at your side no matter what your decision." The woman glanced toward the sleeping Willa. "It's what families do."

"Christ." Indy gave a sharp laugh. "Has there ever been a more dysfunctional bunch?"

Karen's smile faded, her eyes filled with pain. "Yes."

Indy hastily changed the subject. Karen never talked about her life before being captured by the Benson Enterprise goons and Indy never pressed for details.

"You have the cage set up?" she instead demanded.

"I do." Karen shuddered. "Filthy thing."

Karen was the only one of them who could actually touch the metal bars that were laced with malachite. The rest of them had been infected with enough Pantera blood, bone marrow, DNA, and god only knew what else to be able to endure the coppery mineral.

Indy had nearly killed herself trying to salvage the stupid thing from the Haymore Center after it'd burned to the ground.

15

"It's the only thing that will hold a Pantera."

"Yeah." Karen grimaced. "Now we just have to get him in there."

Indy smiled with more confidence than she felt. "Leave that to me."

Karen bit her lower lip. "Indy, I wish you wouldn't go alone."

"This is my responsibility."

"Why do you always take everything on your shoulders?"

"It was my decision to take Willa from the lab." Her stomach twisted with regret. Her impulsive nature wasn't always a good thing. There were times when she made hasty decisions that hurt others. "It's possible that removing her is what made her sick."

Karen shook her head. "It's much more likely that whatever the bastards were infecting her with is what caused the damage."

Indy shrugged. "We won't know until I get the doctor."

Karen narrowed her eyes. "A very smooth sidestep of my question."

Indy held up her hands. It wasn't a sidestep. Or not a deliberate one. The truth was…she didn't really know why she assumed she should be in charge of fixing the world.

She just did.

"It's my responsibility because it's what I do," she muttered.

"Indy?"

The small voice came from the bed and Indy leaned forward to whisper in Karen's ear.

"Get the dart gun from the locker and put it in my backpack," she ordered. "I'm going to speak with Willa before I take off."

Karen gave a reluctant nod, heading out of the room as Indy crossed the cracked and peeling floor to stand next to the bed.

Instinctively her hand reached to push the blond curls from Willa's tiny, heart-shaped face. Although they didn't have an exact date for the child's birth, they assumed she must be around five or six years old.

Too young to have endured being tortured.

"Hey, kitten," she murmured, forcing a smile to her lips even as she took in the child's flushed cheeks and the hectic glitter in the wide hazel eyes.

Willa flashed her dimples. "I'm not a kitten."

"Are you sure?" Indy teased, reaching to brush her fingers over her cheeks, covertly feeling for a fever. She hid her grimace as she felt the heat that radiated from the child's skin. "You have two eyes like a kitty." She grabbed Willa's ears, giving them a light tug. "And two fuzzy ears. And a nose with whiskers—"

"I'm a girl," Willa laughingly protested.

"Ah. So you are," Indy murmured, her fingers pushing the curls from Willa's damp forehead. "The prettiest little girl in the whole world."

"As pretty as Karen?" Willa demanded.

Indy chuckled. "Just as pretty."

"And as smart as Nadia?"

Indy nodded. Nadia was an intensely shy young woman with a self-conscious stutter who Indy had rescued five years before. It was because of her skill with healing that Willa had survived this long.

"Just as smart. And as strong as Tarin," she assured the little girl. "And as loyal as Caleb."

Willa reached up a small hand to touch Indy's cheek. "And as brave as you?"

Indy covered the tiny fingers with her hand, pressing them against her skin.

"There's no need for you to be brave, Willa," she said, the words a solemn oath. "I'm going to take care of you. I promise."

CHAPTER 2

Indy leaned against the rough brick wall of the building, trying to remember how to breathe.

She tried to tell herself that it was fear that was making her heart pound and her palms sweat. She was, after all, creeping through the dark, intent on capturing a lethal male who could kill her without a thought.

But she couldn't lie. Not even to herself.

The sensations jolting through her had nothing to do with fear, and everything to do with shocked fascination.

Good. God.

When she'd trailed the Pantera to his office yesterday it had been from a distance and she'd never actually seen his face.

Tonight, however, she'd arrived at dusk and picked out an emergency exit door that provided a place to hide as well as a full view of the parking lot. Two hours later, Dr. Savary had strolled around the corner of the building with a blond-haired woman clinging to his arm.

Despite the dark, Indy had easily been able to make out the man's exquisitely carved features. The wide brow, the narrow blade of a nose, the high, chiseled cheekbones and the sculpted curve of his lips. His white-gold hair contrasted sharply with dark eyes set beneath thick brows, and the rich bronze of his skin.

She'd never seen such a beautiful male and for a second she found herself dazzled, unable to believe he could be real.

It wasn't until he came to a halt at the edge of the parking lot that she managed to regain control of her sizzling hormones.

Okay, he was gorgeous. And for the first time in her life she was consumed with the need to rip off a man's clothes and lick him from head to toe.

But she couldn't afford to be distracted.

Not when Willa's life hung in the balance.

Hidden in the shadows, she watched as the woman leaned forward, pressing her impressive boobs against the doctor's chest.

"You're sure that you can't join me for dinner?" she purred. "My lasagna is good enough to make grown men cry."

Indy nearly gagged. Was that how a normal woman tried to convince a man to have sex with her?

Yeesh.

"Tempting," the man murmured.

The blond giggled. "What could I offer to make it more tempting?"

His hand lifted to cup her cheek. "Elan, look at me."

She obediently tilted back her head. "Mmm?"

"You will forget about our evening tonight," he ordered in soft tones. "You worked late. Alone."

Indy pressed a hand over her mouth as she watched

the blank expression descend on the woman's pretty face. She'd heard about the Pantera ability to mess with humans' minds, but she'd never seen it in action.

"Alone," the blond repeated.

The doctor turned her toward the parking lot, giving her a gentle push.

"Go home, female."

"Yes," she agreed in wooden tones, walking toward a nearby BMW. "Home."

Dr. Savary remained at the edge of the lot as the woman started her car and drove away. Then he turned, as if he was about to re-enter the hospital. Indy hastily stepped forward. This was her best, and potentially only opportunity to capture the man.

First, however, she had to get close enough to strike.

"Nice trick," she drawled, stepping from the doorway.

He stilled, watching her with the eyes of a predator as she strolled forward.

Heat prickled over her skin despite her leather coat, and her hand instinctively tightened on the dart gun she had hidden in her pocket.

"It's not nice to spy on people," he said on a low growl.

She forced a smile to her lips, trying to ignore the strange awareness racing through her body. It was almost as if there was an electrical current racing between them, zapping her with bolts of excitement.

"It's not nice to screw with their minds either."

His nose flared as he caught her scent, his muscles clenching as he studied her in wary confusion.

21

"Who are you?"

She shrugged, not surprised by his puzzlement. He had to be sensing she wasn't just another harmless human.

Which meant she had only a few seconds left before he decided to figure out exactly what she was.

"Indy," she said, trying to look small and harmless as she took a few more steps forward.

"Just Indy?"

She unconsciously licked her lips. His voice was a low, slow drawl, like melted molasses.

"Just Indy," she rasped.

His gaze darted around the parking lot, his instincts clearly warning him something was wrong.

"Hasn't anyone told you that it's dangerous for a young girl to be out on her own?"

"Are you asking if I'm alone?"

The dark, mesmerizing gaze returned to her pale face. "I was expressing my concern—" His words were cut off as she abruptly jerked her hand from the jacket and aimed the dart gun at the center of his chest. A second later she'd pulled the trigger and he glanced down in shock. "Shit," he breathed.

He managed to take a step backward before he was swaying to the side. Just for a minute he glared at her with stark incredulity, then, with a low groan, he toppled to the hard pavement.

Indy rushed forward, regret twisting her heart.

She knew the malachite she'd shot into his body would cause agonizing pain.

"I really am sorry about this," she muttered, hooking her hands beneath his shoulders and dragging him the short distance to her truck that was parked in a loading dock.

Not for the first time she thanked whatever god might be listening that she was far stronger than a normal woman as she wrestled the unconscious doctor into the back of the truck. Angel might look sleek and lean, but he weighed a freaking ton.

Wiping the sweat from her brow, she glanced around to make sure she hadn't been spotted. When no alarms went off, she climbed into the cab of the vehicle that Tarin had stolen from The Haymore Center and shoved it into gear.

Less than half an hour later she was back at the school and Tarin and Caleb had carried Dr. Savary into the locker room where Karen had set up the cage.

Still on edge, Indy had ordered the boys to go back outside to make sure she hadn't been followed. Not that Tarin would thank her for thinking of him as a boy, she wryly acknowledged. He'd just turned twenty years old and considered himself very much a man.

Crouching beside the cage, she silently studied her prisoner as Karen entered the dilapidated room that'd been stripped bare of everything but a few rusty lockers and an empty shower stall.

"Good god..." the woman breathed, giving a disbelieving shake of her head. "He's magnificent."

Indy rolled her eyes. The man was clearly lethal to poor women.

"Karen," she muttered.

"What?" She gave a helpless shrug. "I'm just saying."

"He's a shifter."

"So what? We're…" The woman gave a vague wave of her hand. "Whatever the hell we are."

"True."

Karen leaned forward, her brow furrowed. "Shouldn't he be awake by now?"

Indy chewed her bottom lip, her gaze locked on the sculpted bronze features that looked disturbingly lifeless.

"I don't know."

"Oh Indy, I hope you didn't truly harm him," Karen breathed, her kind heart unable to bear the thought of anyone being hurt.

"So do I," Indy muttered, pretending to be a true hard-ass even as her gaze was locked on the man sprawled across the cement floor. "There's no way I'll be able to find another Pantera doctor."

Karen sucked in a shocked breath at her callous words. "Indy."

She turned her head to meet her friend's chiding glance, her tension easing as she sensed the Pantera's heartbeat quicken as he started to regain consciousness.

"It's okay, Karen," she soothed the woman. "I stole the darts from our captors' little shop of horrors. The bastards were ruthless, but they wouldn't risk killing their test subjects. The Pantera were too hard to get their hands on."

Karen grimaced. "I hope you're right."

Indy reached to give her friend's hand a comforting squeeze.

"Why don't you make something to eat?" she asked, knowing Karen would feel better if she felt like she was doing something to help. And, of course, it would get Karen out of the room when Dr. Savary fully wakened and condemned them to hell. An inevitable fate that was oddly depressing. "He's going to be hungry when he does wake up."

"Okay." Karen studied her, clearly aware that Indy was trying to get rid of her. "Don't do anything foolish."

Indy watched her friend reluctantly walk out of the locker room, her mouth dry as the air abruptly warmed with the power of the man's frustration.

He might be lying unmoving on the floor, but she could hear the increase in his heartbeat and feel the prickle of energy that told her the creature inside him was alert and dangerously pissed off.

"I know you're awake," she said, relieved when her voice came steady.

There was a brief pause, as if the man was considering his options. Then, clearly realizing he was temporarily trapped, he opened his eyes and shoved himself into a sitting position.

He was pale and a lingering pain was etched onto his elegant features, but his beauty was still breathtaking. Helplessly her gaze skimmed over his hair that shimmered with a pure white-gold beneath the overhead lights and his eyes that studied her with an intense intelligence.

"Congratulations, Indy," he growled, the air vibrating with his barely leashed fury. "It's not often I underestimate the enemy."

She flinched at the mocking derision in his voice before she was tilting her chin to a determined angle.

"I'm not your enemy."

His short, ugly laugh echoed through the air.

"You shot me with a malachite dart and locked me in a cage." He glanced around the depressingly shabby room with its peeling paint and broken window covered by some weird-ass chicken wire. "Trust me, honey, we're enemies."

It shouldn't matter what he thought of her. He was a means to an end. Nothing more than a tool to save Willa.

But suddenly she realized it did matter.

A lot.

"Let me explain."

He leaned against the cot that Karen had placed in the cage, folding his arms over his chest as he stretched out his legs.

"Do I have a choice?"

She slowly rose to her feet. Even though he was caged, the Pantera managed to command the room with the sheer force of his presence.

"What do you know about Stanton Locke?"

He hissed, a low growl rumbling in his chest. "You work for him?"

"Hell no," she denied, her voice harsh. "I was a prisoner in one of the labs he owns."

He tensed, clearly caught off guard by her sharp response. Then…he studied her. Really studied her. Perhaps for the first time.

Something dark and dangerous flared through his eyes, an enticing musk scenting the air before he gave an abrupt shake of his head.

"You're not Pantera."

Her lips twisted at the accusation in his voice. Did he assume that no one but the Pantera had suffered at the hands of Locke and his cronies?

"No. I'm human." She shrugged. "Or at least I was until my mother sold me to Benson Enterprises."

He did another long, disturbingly intense survey of her, sweeping down her taut body before he met her guarded gaze.

"Benson?" he finally demanded and Indy released the breath she hadn't even known she was holding.

She hated trying to explain how any mother could willingly sell her only child to a monster.

"They're a research lab based in New York," she explained.

"It's owned by Locke?"

Indy didn't have to ask the male's opinion of Stanton Locke. The very air sizzled with the force of his seething hatred.

"His name is on the dummy corporation that runs it," she qualified. At the beginning she'd devoted every waking thought to how she could destroy Locke for what he'd done to her and dozens of others. But over the years, she'd uncovered enough evidence to make her realize that Locke was just the tip of the iceberg. "Although I suspect he's nothing more than a flunky for a man, or men, who prefer to hide in the shadows."

His expression was unreadable as he considered her words, but Indy didn't need to be a mind reader to know he remained deeply suspicious of her.

Not to mention...pissed as hell.

Not that she blamed him. But she had to find some way to convince him she had no choice. How else could she plead for him to help Willa?

"While you were at the lab did you see any Pantera being held there?" he abruptly demanded.

"Yes. They were being held in the secret tunnels built beneath the labs," she revealed, a tiny shiver racing through her body at the memory of their agonized cries that echoed through the vents. "The rats were kept a floor above them. I could hear them sometimes. At night."

His brows snapped together. "Rats?"

"The humans, like me, who were kept for experimentation."

***

Angel pressed his hands against the cold cement floor, struggling to remain upright. Fucking malachite. Even though it had burned out of his bloodstream, it still left him feeling weak and dangerously vulnerable.

Even worse, his cat was restless and distracted, prowling beneath his skin as it urged him to break through the bars and reach the female who'd taken him captive.

A reasonable response, if the damned thing was anticipating the taste of her blood. Or the sensation of his claws ripping through her flesh.

She'd tricked him, darted him with a toxic brew of malachite, imprisoned him, and admitted that she knew their enemy, even if she claimed she was as much a victim as the Pantera.

He should be foaming at the mouth to destroy the bitch.

Instead the animal inside him was far more intent

on getting a better sniff of her enticing scent of wildflowers. And licking that creamy smooth skin to see if it was truly as soft as it looked. And getting her pinned beneath him so he could sink into her heat...

Shit.

With an effort he leashed his beast, trying to clear his foggy mind. Later he would worry about his reaction to the tiny, dark-haired female.

For now, he needed to uncover her true connection to Stanton Locke. Maybe she was the victim she claimed to be, or maybe this was just another trap set by their enemies.

Either way, he had to discover what she knew about Locke and his connection to the Pantera.

After that...she belonged to him.

His cat gave a low growl of anticipation. He had every intention of hauling Indy to the Wildlands. Not because he wanted the aggravating female in his homelands and in his power... Okay, that was a lie.

He desperately wanted her in his power.

But most importantly, he couldn't allow a human with the knowledge of malachite to simply roam around. Not until they could be damned sure she wasn't going to reveal the Pantera weakness to others.

But first things first.

"What kind of experimentation?" he demanded, grimly forcing himself to his feet.

"It was different for all of us," she said, her expression distracted as she became lost in the past. "Karen was a brood mare."

Angel's brows snapped together. Was she implying what he thought she was implying?

"What's that mean?"

"She was inseminated with Pantera sperm."

Angel's hands curled into tight fists. Yep. It was exactly what he feared.

Dammit. They'd been searching for additional property that Locke might own, but Angel had fiercely hoped the Haymore Center had been his only Frankenstein laboratory.

"She became pregnant?"

Indy glanced toward the door of the locker room, as if ensuring they were alone. Angel abruptly realized that she was talking about the female he'd sensed in the room before he'd opened his eyes.

"Several times," she admitted in clipped tones. "Most ended in miscarriages, but she managed to go full term for three children."

"What happened to them?"

"The two older boys were taken away before I could help her escape." Her stunning eyes darkened to deep shade of indigo, her anger heating the air just as if she was a Pantera. Odd. "We did manage to save her younger son, Caleb. We're still searching for the older ones."

He took a step forward, fascinated by her obvious frustration. This was a female who not only cared about others, but took an active role as a protector.

"Were you a brood mare?"

"No." She gave a sharp shake of her head, the silky ebony strands falling across her forehead. "I was a cavy."

A nasty sense of dread clenched his stomach. He was a doctor. He knew exactly what a 'cavy' meant.

"A test subject," he said in flat tones.

She wrapped her arms around her slender waist, her cocky bravado missing as she visibly struggled with the demons from her past.

"Exactly," she rasped.

Angel could sense the truth of her words. Her pain was too raw, too soul-deep to be faked. Not that he trusted her. There wasn't a chance in hell he was letting down his guard until he had the female locked in his home in the Wildlands. But he was beginning to accept that she truly had been tortured by Locke.

"What did they do to you?"

"I'm not entirely sure." She grimaced. "Layton was given blood transfusions with Pantera blood—"

"Layton?" he sharply interrupted. The male had better hope he didn't have a claim on this female.

"One of the young men I rescued from the New York lab," she explained, her tone one of an older sister instead of a lover. "Along with Nadia, who was given a bone marrow transplant."

Angel sucked in a harsh breath. "Christ."

She hunched a shoulder, her expression defensive as if uncomfortable at the thought he might feel sorry for her. Something dangerous tightened his chest. Not just his cat that was raging with the need to punish anyone stupid enough to hurt this female, but a strange sensation that was all human and all male.

"I was always unconscious when they took me from my cage into the lab, but I suspect they somehow screwed with my DNA," she admitted in harsh tones.

Angel grimly leashed his perilously intense reaction to this female and instead forced himself to concentrate on her confession.

31

"Why do you think they did something to your DNA?"

She shivered, no doubt reacting to his barely contained fury.

"I'm stronger than most women and faster. I can also see in the dark."

Angel narrowed his gaze. "And you can sense Pantera?" he pressed.

"How did…" Her startled words broke off as she grimaced, realizing she'd given herself away. "Yes."

"What else?"

"I can also sense cavies."

He frowned. If she could sense the lab rats then she had to have even more Pantera blood than he'd first suspected.

Damn.

"Any other gifts?"

Her lips twisted with a bitterness she made no effort to hide. "Gifts? Is that a joke?" she snapped. "I've been cursed, Dr. Savary."

He stepped forward, halting just inches from the bars that were laced with malachite.

"Angel," he corrected with a soft growl.

She frowned. "What?"

"My name is Angel."

Her gaze swept over his face, a faint blush of arousal touching her cheeks even as she sent him a taunting smile.

"Did you give yourself that nickname?" she demanded.

"No." He hid his amusement at her ridiculous attempt to pretend indifference. Who did she think she was fooling? The air sizzled between them. Heat. Desire. Hunger. She was being consumed by the merciless awareness that burned between them. "The day I was born my mother took one look at me and announced I was as beautiful as an Angel."

She wrinkled her nose. "Yeesh."

He shrugged. "You asked."

"I thought it was ridiculous my mother named me Tuesday because that's the day she had me."

He stilled, suspicion making his hands clench. "I thought you said your name was Indy?"

"My mother called me Tuesday. After she sold me, I was taken to the clinic and my captors called me Patient F." She gave a defiant toss of her head, the courage it'd taken to survive her harsh life etched on her face. "When I finally escaped I named myself Independence. It was Caleb who shortened it to Indy."

Angel released his breath on a low hiss. God. Damn. This woman was…special.

Sensing her pride would rebel at any hint of sympathy, he instead concentrated on the men who'd hurt her.

He had every intention of destroying them.

"Tell me more about the lab."

She stepped toward the cage, the scent of wildflowers spicing the air.

"I'll answer any questions you have after you do something for me."

Ah. So at last they came to the reason she'd taken the extreme risk of capturing him.

About damned time.

"What?"

She licked her lips, looking astonishingly young and vulnerable despite the biker outfit.

"Six months ago I got a lead on the Haymore Center," she said, her voice strained. "We hoped we could track down one of Karen's sons."

Angel studied Indy's tense features. She was afraid. But not for herself.

"I'm assuming they weren't here?"

"No." Her gaze darted toward the door before returning to meet his unreadable expression. "I did, however, manage to sneak out a young girl we named Willa."

Angel felt a stab of surprise. They'd searched the center before it'd burned to the ground. Had she gotten the child out before they arrived?

"She was in the lab?" he demanded.

Indy shook her head. "Actually we found her in an annex two blocks from the center."

He barely resisted the urge to pull out the cellphone that was strapped to his ankle along with a lethal dagger. Whoever had frisked him before tossing him in the cage had done a piss-poor job. They'd found and disposed of the phone he used when he was dealing with hospital business, but failed to continue the search. Sloppy. When he had Indy in the Wildlands, he would teach her how to do a thorough frisk. A slow, delectable frisk that would end when they were both naked and he was buried deep inside her.

"Parish is going to have a shit fit when he realizes we overlooked an annex," he growled.

She shook her head. "There's nothing to overlook. It burnt to the ground last week."

Of course it did.

Locke was nothing if not brutally methodical in covering his tracks.

His lips flattened as he felt a burst of impatience to be out of the cage.

"You still haven't told me why you're holding me like I'm an animal."

She bit her bottom lip, something that might have been regret darkening her stunning blue eyes.

"I need you to save Willa."

"You said you rescued her."

"I did. But now she's sick. Unless you can help her I'm afraid—"

Her words trailed away and Angel realized she was afraid the little girl was going to die.

Abruptly Angel was all business.

He was a Healer. It didn't matter if his patient was Pantera, human or some strange mixture in between.

"Take me to her," he commanded.

Reaching into the pocket of her jacket, she pulled out a small dart gun and pointed it at the center of his heart.

"Let's go."

CHAPTER 3

Indy knew that the Pantera walking at her side was furious.

Not only was the air sizzling with the heat of his cat, but his obscenely beautiful face was tight with an expression that warned of retribution.

Still, what choice did she have?

He seemed to believe her claim that she was as much a victim of Locke as his precious Pantera, but for all she knew it was nothing more than an act to make her lower her guard. She had to assume he was going to do everything in his power to escape.

Right?

Unfortunately, Angel wasn't impressed by her need for caution. His accusing eyes had never wavered from her face as she'd carefully unlocked the door and moved to shove the gun into his side.

In tense silence they'd left the locker room, stepping over the rubble that littered the hallway. The entire building was a deathtrap, but until Willa was better she couldn't risk dragging her to New York.

Urging him into the nurse's office, she pressed the dart gun even harder into his side.

"Remember, if you try anything I'll zap you," she warned in low tones.

Turning his head he regarded her with eyes that held the golden power of his cat.

Angry. Ruthless. And unnervingly patient.

A predator willing to wait for the kill.

"I won't forget, honey." He bent his head to whisper directly into her ear. "Not a damned thing."

She didn't even bother trying to hide her shiver of unease. Or was it arousal?

More than likely it was a toxic combination of both.

"Willa is across the room," she muttered.

Slowly he lifted his head, his hair shimmering with the purity of platinum. Sucking in a deep breath, he used his heightened senses to sort through the various scents.

He made a sound of shock as he jerked his head to the side, studying her with an accusing glare.

"She smells like Pantera."

"I know," she swiftly agreed. "But she's human."

"You're sure?"

She gave a firm nod. Over the years she'd become an expert at being able to detect the subtle differences between a born Pantera and one that'd been created by transfusions or insemination.

Tarin called it her 'super-power.'

"Yes."

There was a faint rustle of cotton sheets, before the soft sound of a young girl's voice was floating across the room.

"Indy?"

Keeping a wary eye on Angel, she crossed the room, half expecting him to bolt. Instead, he moved to the bed with long, confident strides.

Breathing a silent sigh of relief, Indy allowed herself to glance down at the tiny girl who barely made a bump beneath the thin blanket.

Her heart squeezed with fear at the sight of the too-pale face and the overly bright eyes. God almighty. This beautiful child was slipping away and there wasn't a damned thing she could do to help her...

No. Wait. That wasn't true.

She'd done the one and only thing in her power to save this precious soul.

"Hey, kitten," she murmured, reaching to tap Willa on the tip of her nose. "I brought someone to see you."

Her eyes widened with excitement, although she was too weak to lift her head off the pillow.

"Who?"

"Angel," the Pantera murmured, taking the last step so he was in Willa's line of vision.

Willa blinked in wonderment, openly enchanted by the male's splendid beauty.

"You're an angel?" she breathed.

The Pantera's lips twitched. "Something like that."

Indy snorted, wondering if there was any woman immune to the male.

Ignoring the dart gun that Indy kept pressed against his side, Angel leaned over the edge of the bed, his expression oddly gentle.

"May I touch you?"

Willa cringed back. No one knew precisely what the poor child had endured in the Haymore Center, but the memories were enough to make her wake up screaming in fear.

"Will it hurt?" she asked.

Heat blasted through the air as Angel realized that Willa had been tortured, but his expression never changed.

"No, little one," he promised, his voice husky. "I swear it won't hurt."

"It's okay, Willa," Indy assured the girl.

Willa gave a slow nod. "'Kay."

Taking care not to press against her fragile body, Angel ran his fingers over her arms and down her legs before he concentrated on her torso.

Indy kept a careful watch on him, not entirely sure what he was doing. She'd heard the Pantera healers had a mystic talent, but she didn't know how it worked. Hell, she wasn't even certain it could help a child who was human.

Angel's expression was distracted as his hands moved to brush over her cheeks.

"Do you hurt anywhere?"

"Sometimes my head hurts. And—" Willa's words broke off as she glanced toward Indy.

"You can tell him," Indy urged.

Willa instinctively tugged the blanket up to her nose. The little girl had learned to protect herself from the open derision when she confessed the truth.

"There's something inside me," she whispered.

Angel leaned forward, his dark eyes glowing with a golden light.

"Inside?"

"It's a voice, but not a voice," Willa reluctantly admitted. "It shows me pictures."

Indy placed her hand on Willa's leg, prepared to shoot the dart if Angel mocked the child's fearful confession.

Of course he didn't. Instead he leaned even closer to the child, his beautiful face intent as he studied Willa.

"Do you remember the pictures?" he asked.

Willa gave a hesitant nod. "Sometimes I'm lying in the sun surrounded by plants. And sometimes I'm running so fast it tickles my ears. And sometimes—" Once again her words broke off, an embarrassed color staining her cheeks.

"Go on, little one," Angel insisted.

"Sometimes I'm biting the bad men who hurt me," Willa confessed in a breathless rush.

Angel flashed a reassuring smile, his fingers brushing through her pale curls.

"You did very good, Willa," he praised as he straightened.

Indy gave the girl's leg a soft squeeze. "She's a good kitten, aren't you?"

"Cat," Angel breathed.

Indy sent him a frown. "What?"

His features hardened with a grim determination. "We need to talk."

Oh…shit.

Indy's heart plummeted as she easily read his concern. He'd been able to sense something about Willa. Something that wasn't good.

"Okay," she muttered, pasting a smile to her lips as she moved to place a soft kiss on Willa's forehead. "I'll send Nadia in to help you with your bath."

Willa's gaze clung to Angel. "Will you come back to visit?"

Angel gave a slow, solemn dip of his head. "I would be honored to visit again."

Sensing she'd earned yet another conquest, Willa gave a bat of her long lashes.

"With cookies?"

Angel tilted back his head as he released a burst of laughter. Indy's breath lodged painfully in her lungs, her entire body going up in flames at the sight of his genuine amusement.

Yeesh. He was gorgeous when he was broody. And when he was mad. And when he was ready to wring her throat.

But he was devastating as his eyes sparkled with wicked humor and his lips parted to reveal snowy white teeth. Teeth she suddenly wanted to feel nibbling at her flesh, stirring the passions she hadn't even known she possessed.

She shuddered, deeply relieved he was still concentrating on Willa.

"You're going to be a very dangerous female, little one," he assured her.

Willa gave a proud nod. "Just like Indy."

The dark eyes slid in her direction, lingering on her flushed face with an intensity that made her mouth go dry.

"Yes, just like Indy," he murmured.

She flattened her lips, fiercely trying to pretend

her stomach wasn't fluttering as a surge of tingling excitement exploded through her.

Dammit. She brought this male here to help Willa, not to stir up sensations that were better left unstirred.

"Let's go," she ordered in abrupt tones, not surprised when he sent her a taunting glance.

A part of her suspected that she wasn't nearly as in control of the situation as he was allowing her to believe. A suspicion that only deepened as he prowled next to her, his graceful movements doing nothing to hide the power beneath his pretense of civilization.

Beneath the expensive clothing and polished air of a professional lurked a primitive hunter just waiting for his opportunity to pounce.

Reaching the hallway, she paused for the dark-haired Nadia to dart past them, her head bent to hide her face. Then, closing the door to the nurse's office, she forced herself to ask the question that she dreaded.

"Do you know what's wrong with her?"

Angel didn't hesitate. "She needs to go to the Wildlands."

Indy stiffened. Okay. That was the last thing she expected. As far as she knew, no humans had ever been invited into the secluded bayous the Pantera called home.

"Why?"

He glanced toward the closed door. "The magic there is the only thing that will heal her."

Indy parted her lips only to snap them shut as she abruptly realized what he was doing. Sharp-edged disappointment lanced through her. Not just because of Willa. But because...

She grimaced, silently admitting the truth.

Over the past hour she'd started to hope he would forget…well, everything. That he'd been shot, kidnapped, and held captive. She wanted him to *want* to help Willa. Unfair? Yeah. But after spending a lifetime dealing with ruthless villains, she wanted a hero.

"Shit. I should have known you would try to play me," she muttered, shaking her head in disgust. "I always heard the Pantera were only concerned with their own people and the hell with the rest of us, but I didn't think you would be so selfish you'd put your needs above that of a sick little girl."

Without warning he was bending down until their noses were nearly touching, the air snapping with the force of his anger.

"Don't presume for a second that you know me or my people, female," he snarled. "You asked me to help Willa and I told you what you need to do."

She wanted to back away. Standing so close she could sense his cat lurking just beneath the surface, its hunger almost palpable. It made the hair rise on the back of her neck.

Indy, however, grimly stood her ground.

She didn't have much in this world, but the one thing she had in spades was courage.

Or, as Karen would call it, bull-headed stubbornness.

"And your prescription is the Wildlands?" She gave a sharp laugh. "The one place you're certain to escape while the rest of us get turned into cat food?"

"I don't have to escape." His voice was filled

with a ruthless assurance that sent a chill down her spine. "I can promise you that a dozen Hunters are already searching for me. I give you one hour, maybe two, before they pick up my trail."

Indy unconsciously licked her lips. He sounded so certain.

"You don't scare me," she forced herself to mutter.

A dangerous smile curved his lips. "Then you're a fool. My brothers won't stop until they have me back." He paused, his gaze taking a slow, thorough survey of her rigid body as he moved to tower over her. "And then you'll be all mine, honey."

An intoxicating musk laced the air, clouding her mind with all sorts of sinful thoughts. Thoughts that included tilting her head to press her lips against the tempting fullness of his mouth. And ripping off that soft cashmere sweater so she could nibble a path down his chest. And running her fingers through the silken platinum of his hair.

Almost as if sensing the treacherous ache that was spreading through her body, Angel moved forward, easily herding her against the dented lockers that lined the hallway.

Her heart thundered, but it wasn't from fear.

Desperate to regain command of the situation, Indy lifted her hand and jabbed him with the tip of the dart gun.

"Back off," she rasped.

He pushed forward, trapping her with the heavy strength of his body.

"Don't worry," he whispered, lowering his head

to stroke a rough tongue down the line of her jaw. He chuckled when he felt her tremble at the tiny shocks of pleasure racing through her. "When I make you my cat food I'll do enough licking up and down this delectable body, you won't mind at all when I start feasting on you." He nipped the lobe of her ear. "In fact, you'll be begging."

***

Six blocks from the abandoned school, Stanton Locke entered the small, private house that was guarded by layers of security. Not that many people would be interested in the plain, three-story brick house in the quiet neighborhood.

Set back from the tree-lined street, it had a high hedge and sturdy gate that prevented the casual pedestrian from getting more than a brief glance of the covered porch.

Laying his hand on the palm scanner that was hidden next to the door, Stanton Locke waited for alarms to disengage before entering the shadowed foyer.

He was a tall man with a lean, distinguished face and brilliant blue eyes. Currently his dark hair was pulled into a short tail at his nape and his slender form attired in a smoke-gray Gucci suit.

At a glance, most people assumed he was a wealthy businessman who had been born to a family of privilege and graduated from Oxford or Yale. Few would ever suspect that he'd been born in the gutters of London. Or that he now was in charge of a vast criminal underworld.

Climbing the steps to the porch, Stanton nodded toward the guard who was seated next to the window overlooking the front yard and stepped into the living room.

An empty living room.

He grimaced. No big surprise. The woman he was seeking rarely watched TV or lounged on the deeply cushioned couches he'd personally picked out for her comfort. She also ignored the kitchen he'd had remodeled in the hope she would enjoy cooking.

Instead Chelsea spent the bulk of her time in the library, hiding from the world in the same way she used to hide behind her science.

That's how they met, in fact.

She was a brilliant genetic researcher who'd worked at Haymore Center until she'd developed cold feet and tried to quit. Unfortunately for her, Stanton's master didn't accept resignations. Once you were included in the inner circle it was a lifetime commitment.

The only way out was death.

Stanton had been ordered to oversee her termination, but for the first time since his master had rescued him from the streets, Stanton had deliberately disobeyed a direct command. There was no way in hell he was hurting Chelsea.

Instead he'd whisked her to this house to keep her hidden from those who would destroy her just to gain an advantage with the master.

Not that she'd appreciated his efforts, he wryly acknowledged, climbing the staircase to the third floor that'd been converted to a massive library. He entered

46

the room that was lined with floor-to-ceiling bookshelves on three walls, with one wall dominated by a dormer window that overlooked the garden in the back.

The ceiling was lofted with open beams that gave the illusion of space, along with light ivory carpeting on the wooden planks.

Moving forward, he at last spotted Chelsea curled in a leather wingback chair near the window.

The early morning sunlight danced over the crimson flames in her long red hair and emphasized the pale ivory of her skin. At his entrance she lifted her head from the book that was opened on her lap, her pale green eyes watching his approach with an unreadable expression.

At the same time, her hair slid away from her face, revealing the scarred flesh that ran from mid-cheek down the side of her throat. The terrible burn that had happened when she was in a fire as a teenager was a jarring contrast to the perfection of her beauty, but unlike Chelsea, Stanton had never thought of it as ugly. To him it was a badge of courage for what she'd suffered.

"I thought you left New Orleans with the Pantera," she said, her voice cold.

Stanton flinched. Once her voice had been laced with a warmth and tenderness that only occurred between lovers.

"I did." His own voice held a British accent he'd honed until it sounded as if he'd attended a posh boarding school.

"Ah..." A mocking resignation settled around

47

her. "Now that you have Hiss safely hidden away, I assume you came back to tidy up loose ends?"

Pain lanced through him, his gaze greedily skimming down her slender body that was attired in casual slacks and a cream cardigan. Once he would have crossed the room and scooped her up in his arms. She would have giggled as he carried her to the leather couch in the corner and kissed her into hot, willing submission.

"In a manner of speaking," he muttered. In truth, he didn't have one damned reason to be in New Orleans. The businesses attached to his name had all been torched and the prisoners moved to a new location.

All but one.

This one…

Perhaps sensing his unease, Chelsea put aside the book, lifting her chin as he stepped forward.

"Will you at least make it quick?"

He frowned at her odd words. "Make what quick?"

"My death."

He sucked in a shocked breath, feeling as if he'd been punched in the gut. Was this truly what they'd come to?

That she could believe he would ever hurt her?

"I'm not going to kill you," he rasped.

She shrugged, slowly rising to her feet. "I'm a loose end. What else are you going to do with me?"

He scowled, deeply offended by her accusation. Had he ever done anything but try to protect her? Even when he knew he risked his own life to keep her hidden.

"How can you ask me that question?" he demanded.

"Don't pretend to be offended, Locke," Chelsea taunted, giving a toss of her head. "We both know you have no morals." Her lips twisted in a humorless smile as her hand reached up to touch her scarred features. "Of course, people in glass houses shouldn't throw stones. I allowed my own vanity to lead me down the pathway to hell."

He crossed the floor, grabbing her hands in a tight grip.

Chelsea had agreed to help with the Pantera project in hopes that the healing properties of their blood would erase the scars that marred her face. Unfortunately, she didn't realize she was making a deal with the devil until too late.

"None of it was what I wanted."

Her lips twisted. "Of course it was."

"No. I've only done what was asked of me," he insisted in harsh tones.

"Don't..." She pulled her hands free, glaring at him with blatant censure. "At least be honest about your lack of conscience. You've killed and tortured and held innocents captive for your own gain."

Stanton grimaced. Okay. He couldn't deny her accusation. He might not be the one ultimately in charge, but he was far from innocent.

"You're right. I sold my soul." His jaw tightened. "But that doesn't mean I haven't had regrets."

Chelsea heaved a sigh, her expression softening with regret. "Too late."

Stanton reached to lightly cup her scarred cheek. "Is it?"

"What?"

"Is it too late?"

She carefully inspected his taut features, searching for…something.

"Have you left your beloved master?" she at last demanded.

His heart fractured. It was the only thing she'd ever asked of him. And the one thing he could never give her.

"No. I can't," he muttered, wishing she could understand. "I owe him too much to walk away."

Her lips flattened. It was an old argument that had torn them apart.

"What do you owe him?"

"I was starving in the street," he said, leaving out the nastier parts of his childhood. Like the bastard who'd pimped him out from the age of five. And the younger brother he'd watched beaten to death by a local gang. "Without my master I would have died."

She released an explosive breath, refusing to accept his belief that he owed his master his unwavering loyalty.

"Foster parents do that every day without expectation of their children becoming their devoted slaves."

"He did more than save me," he insisted, his thumb rubbing her full bottom lip. "He educated me and gave me a life of luxury."

"And that's so important to you?"

Her simple question squeezed the air from his lungs. Until Chelsea, everything had been easy.

His master told him what needed to be done, and he did it. No fuss. No muss.

He didn't have to consider tedious things like right or wrong. Or the pain he was causing others.

"It was." His fingers tightened on her cheek, an acute longing twisting his gut. "Now…"

"Now what?" she prompted when his words trailed away.

"Now I fear my purpose in life was nothing more than an illusion."

Her hand lifted to lie against his chest, the light touch sending jolts of pleasure through him.

"Locke?"

His lips twitched. He loved that she always called him by his last name. Even when she was wrapped in his arms.

"What am I going to do with you?" he muttered.

***

Angel considered himself a civilized male.

He might be Pantera, but he refused to be ruled by his primitive instincts. Instead he used cold logic to rule his life. Even his skill as a Healer was used in combination with hard science and human technology.

But pacing the cage he felt anything but civilized.

Maybe he should have listened to Raphael. When Angel had made a hurried call to the Wildlands, the older male had insisted he make his escape and wait for Parish and his Hunters to arrive so they could round up the strange collection of humans.

Angel, however, found himself unable to leave.

He was waiting for…what?

The question was churning through his mind

when there was the sound of footsteps and a human male with tousled black hair and eyes that were puma gold stepped into the room. Angel instantly moved toward the door of the cage, his senses absorbing the male's peculiar scent. He was human. But there was a distinct musk that was pure cat.

"Who are you?" Angel demanded.

"Tarin." Warily crossing the room, the male bent down to shove a tray of food beneath the bars. "I brought you breakfast."

Angel's stomach rumbled. How long had it been since he'd eaten? Seven or eight hours?

His true hunger, however, wasn't for food.

"Where's Indy?" he sharply demanded.

In an effort to hide his nerves, Tarin wiped his hands down the front of his jeans that were nearly as threadbare as his New York Giants sweatshirt.

"She's eating with Willa."

His lips twisted. "Coward."

Tarin frowned, misreading Angel's annoyance that the female was trying to avoid him.

"I hope you won't judge her too harshly."

Angel narrowed his gaze. "I admire your loyalty, but what happens between Indy and myself is no one's business."

The male scowled, easily picking up on Angel's possessive tone.

"Indy will go to any lengths to save one of her kids."

Angel sucked in a sharp breath. "Willa's…?"

"Not her biological child," Tarin swiftly denied. "But Indy has some sort of savior complex that drives her to risk her idiotic neck over and over when she knows someone is in danger."

An odd combination of pride and gut-clenching fear raced through Angel at the thought of the female's daring rescue missions.

"She helped you escape?" he demanded.

"Yes." Tarin nodded. "I was a cavy in the Benson horror show."

With an effort Angel squashed the thought of Indy deliberately putting herself in danger. It was too...disturbing. Instead he concentrated on the young male who had firsthand knowledge of Locke's lab.

"What did they do to you?"

Tarin stiffened, his face tight with remembered pain. "I was given transfusions."

"With Pantera blood?"

"Yeah."

Angel frowned. Because of Lydia they knew that the Haymore Center had been used to impregnate human women with Pantera sperm. But they hadn't realized there'd been secret experimentations with injecting humans with blood, bone marrow, and the Goddess knew what else.

"Did your captors say why?"

For a long, tense moment Angel thought the younger male might refuse to answer. Then, with a restless shrug, he paced across the floor.

"They would injure me and then give me the blood to see if it would help me heal."

"Shit," Angel breathed, comprehension slamming into him with the force of a freight train.

Their enemies had been experimenting with

Pantera blood to determine if they could use it for their own gain. Why hadn't the Pantera suspected that from the start?

"Did it accelerate your healing?"

Tarin continued to pace, his face averted as if he was ashamed of what the humans had done to him.

"It cured the diseases they infected me with and most of the physical wounds they inflicted."

A fiery hatred scorched through Angel. What sort of twisted sicko would kidnap vulnerable children and abuse them as if they were no more than caged rodents?

"Those bastards," he snarled, the human part of him as anxious as his cat to spill blood. Locke and his followers were evil. Pure and simple. "I'll kill them."

Tarin halted, turning to meet Angel's burning gaze.

"Indy already did," the younger male informed him. "Or at least the two guards who got their jollies by slicing me open and seeing how long they could make me suffer before giving me the blood." Tarin shuddered, his eyes glowing gold. "I knew one day they'd go too far. That I'd die before they could heal me." He held up his hand as Angel's lips parted to interrupt. "And then Indy came," he said, his devotion to the courageous female etched on his face. "She took two bullets before she got me out of there, but she didn't complain once."

Angel's mouth went dry, his cat roaring in fury. Indy had been shot. She might have died before he ever met her.

Unacceptable.

Clearly she needed someone to protect her.

"You don't have to worry," he assured his captor. "My family is going to track them down and destroy each and every one of them."

Tarin didn't look particularly impressed by the promise.

"That's fine, but don't forget it wasn't your family who got us out of the labs or captured a full-grown Pantera just because she was worried about Willa," he said, folding his arms over his chest. "That was all Indy."

CHAPTER 4

Indy prided herself on her courage.

Her mother had broken her heart. Her captors had broken her body. But by god, no one was going to break her spirit.

Or at least that's what she'd always told herself.

She couldn't, however, deny that it was pure cowardice that'd kept her away from the Pantera currently residing in the locker room.

It wasn't that she feared for her safety. He was, after all, safely locked in a cage. He couldn't physically hurt her. But he disturbed her in a way that was downright embarrassing.

He was her prisoner. A tool to help Willa.

She wasn't supposed to be lusting over him like an overly hormonal teenager.

Unfortunately, her body didn't agree. Even after she'd left him in the locker room she could catch the enticing scent of his musk clinging to her body, as if he'd managed to mark her on some primitive level. And worse, when she'd stretched out on her narrow cot to try and get an hour of much needed sleep, her dreams had been consumed by X-rated fantasies of the gorgeous male.

Which was why she'd sent the breakfast tray with Tarin instead of facing the prisoner who was forcing her to confront needs she'd managed to keep buried for years.

Now entering the locker room to see Tarin's eyes glowing with suppressed emotions, she felt a stab of guilt. Dammit, she should never have exposed the young man to the full-blooded Pantera.

"Caleb's looking for you, Tarin," she said in gentle tones. "I think he had a bad morning."

Tarin instantly turned to send her a worried glance. "He can feel the Pantera."

Angel made a sound of shock. "What did you say?"

Tarin turned to meet Angel's disbelieving gaze. "Caleb said it's like being near a tuning fork that keeps vibrating deep inside him."

"Take him to Nadia," Indy commanded. The young woman could soothe most aches and pains. "Maybe she can help."

Tarin's expression hardened. "Indy, you shouldn't be alone with—"

"I'm not going to do anything to hurt her," Angel abruptly intruded into the younger male's protest. "I swear."

"Go on, Tarin," Indy urged, glaring at her prisoner. She didn't need him making worthless promises. "I can take care of myself."

With a grudging nod Tarin headed out of the locker room, the sound of his footsteps echoing through the heavy silence.

Indy's attention never wavered from the large,

painfully beautiful male who was watching her with a small, disturbingly smug smile.

"So you think you can take care of yourself?"

Indy jutted her chin. Okay, he was edible. And her body was tingling with a treacherous heat. But she didn't let anyone treat her like she was some helpless bimbo.

"Yes."

His smile widened. "I wouldn't be so sure about that."

Stepping forward he grasped the bars of the cage and shoved the door open.

Indy blinked. Then blinked again. That shouldn't be possible. The cages were specifically built to hold Pantera.

Had the fire somehow altered the malachite in the bars? Or had she simply gotten ahold of a defective cage?

The inane thoughts were shattered as she belatedly realized that she had a full-grown Pantera male stalking toward her with grim intent.

Oh...shit.

With a muffled cry, Indy turned and darted toward the door. She was too late. A step from escape she felt herself being scooped off the ground and tossed over Angel's broad shoulder.

Furious with her stupidity in letting down her guard, Indy beat her fists against his back. It didn't even occur to her to scream. There no way she was putting any of the others in danger.

She'd already done quite enough...thank you very fucking much.

Intent on thumping her hands against his rock-hard muscles, she didn't pay attention to where they were headed. Not until she heard a door slam and lock before he was lowering her to her feet.

A hasty glance revealed they were in a small office that had remarkably avoided the worst of the hurricane damage. The windows were intact, along with a heavy desk and two chairs and a row of file cabinets. The walls were peeling, but the linoleum floor had only small cracks.

Most importantly, it had only one exit.

And a very large, very dangerous Pantera was blocking it.

Indy scrambled backward. Screw her pride. Right now all that mattered was getting some distance between her and the male she'd kidnapped and held prisoner.

"What are you doing?" she demanded.

Angel leaned against the closed door, folding his arms over his chest. Then, lifting his hands, he slowly peeled off the thin surgical gloves that the bastard had no doubt stolen from the nurse's office.

Shit.

That's how he managed to endure touching the malachite.

"We're going to talk."

"Okay."

She forced a smile to her lips even as her hand crept behind her. She'd stuffed her phone in the back pocket of her jeans. If she could get it pulled out far enough she could call 911…

There was a muttered curse before Angel was moving toward her with a blinding speed. Indy barely had time to process the fact he was standing directly in front of her before she felt the phone being snatched out of her hand and tossed against the wall with enough force to shatter it into a hundred pieces.

"Don't be an idiot," Angel growled.

Indy snapped her head up, her fear forgotten as a burst of fury raced through her.

"You're pissing me off," she snapped.

"Welcome to the club, honey." He glared down at her, his sculpted features tight as he battled back an intense emotion.

Anger? Frustration? Hunger?

She licked her suddenly dry lips. "I was only trying to help Willa."

"I know." His brooding gaze lowered to her lips as he lifted his hand to brush the back of his fingers over her cheek and down the curve of her throat. Almost as if he was fascinated by the feel of her skin. "It's the only reason I didn't take off the second the malachite was burned from my system."

She shivered, his light touch making her stomach clench with excitement.

"The gloves…"

Her words trailed away as his fingers brushed over the sensitive skin at her nape before plunging into her hair. Giving a light tug, he angled her head back, forcing her to meet the smoldering heat in his dark eyes.

"Yeah, you really should pay more attention to your prisoner," he murmured, his tone distracted.

"Fine. I'm an idiot." She tried to hold on to her anger. It was that or melt into a puddle of aching need at his feet. "Why don't you leave?"

"Because you and your people have information we need."

Her treacherous desire was momentarily forgotten as she realized what her impetuous decision to kidnap a Pantera had truly accomplished.

"Dammit," she breathed. "Karen was right."

His fingers stroked through her hair, his gaze still locked on her lips.

"Right about what?"

She tried to think, but suddenly the room felt way too small. Or maybe it was just Angel who was way too close. Either way, the force of his presence was making it impossible to clear her mind.

"I put everyone in danger," she at last managed to mutter.

His brows snapped together, as if he was annoyed by her stumbled words.

"Stop that," he growled. "No one's in danger," he denied. "And you saved Willa."

Had she? She desperately wanted to cling to his words. It was unbearable to think that the little girl couldn't be cured.

"What are you going to do?"

"Take her to the Wildlands," he answered without hesitation. "The magic there is the only thing that will heal her."

"You swear?"

"I swear."

She studied the male face, struggling to resist the temptation to trace each perfect feature. Sometimes she wasn't sure he could be real.

Her hand was actually lifting when she abruptly

came to her senses. With a small shake of her head, she met his gaze that glowed with the power of his cat in the morning light.

She needed to get away from this male. He made her feel weak and vulnerable and dangerously needy.

Emotions she couldn't afford if she was to continue her crusade.

"I want to say goodbye to her," she muttered.

"There's no need."

She stiffed. "But—"

"You're going with her."

She stared at him in disbelief. Go to the Wildlands? Become a captive of the mysterious shifters?

Be with this male every day and night…

Oh no. Hell, no.

"Thanks, but I'll take a hard pass on that," she said in dry tones.

His fingers slid through her hair and down her nape, at last circling her throat.

"I'm not asking you, honey," he murmured softly. "I'm telling you."

She should have been terrified. This large male could break her neck and hide her body in the rubble in the blink of an eye. But it wasn't fear that was making her heart pound and her breath rasp past her parted lips. Instead, it was the heated musk that was stroking over her skin like a caress.

"It's not your call," she tried to bluff.

He studied her pale features. "I think you'll find that it is."

"Angel."

A low rumble vibrated in his chest. "I like my name on your lips." His gaze lowered to her mouth, his eyes smoldering with a golden hunger. "Of course, I think there're a lot of things I'm going to like on your lips."

Stark, ruthless need blazed through her at the mere suggestion of kissing a path over his bare chest and down to the thick cock that was pressed against her lower stomach.

She'd needed to taste him. To feel his heat searing away the chill that'd haunted her since her mother had sold her like a piece of unwanted property.

She'd never ached for anyone or anything so badly in her entire life.

Which only reinforced her need to get as far away from this male as possible.

"Have you lost your mind?" she forced herself to mutter.

"Yes."

***

Indy blinked at his blunt honesty. "Well...I..." She licked her lips. "That would explain several things."

Angel grinned at her unexpected hint of bewilderment. He was a Pantera alpha. Her reckless courage was like an aphrodisiac. What other woman would have battled their enemy so boldly?

But there was something very sexy in that brief glimpse of vulnerability.

Rubbing his thumb up and down the side of her throat, he surveyed her pale, perfect features. Even wearing the oversized leather jacket and her face smudged with dust, she was still the most beautiful creature he had ever seen.

"Do you ever give an inch, Indy?" he said softly.

She held his searching gaze. "Do you?"

"Never." He smiled with slow anticipation. "It should make our relationship interesting."

"Relationship?" Her eyes widened, but before she could speak, he had his arms wrapped around her waist and was jerking her against his chest.

With the patience of a Hunter, Angel waited until her lips parted in protest before he lowered his head to claim them in a rough kiss.

She made a strangled sound of shock. He didn't blame her. He was a shitload of dazed and confused himself. How many females had been eager to crawl into his bed over the past century? Dozens. Hundreds. But no matter how flagrantly they'd tried to attract his attention, he'd never made a habit of grabbing and kissing them like he truly was an animal.

So why did Indy provoke him to a near violent urge to possess her?

A part of him feared the answer.

Okay, he desired her. He craved her with a force that was rapidly becoming an obsession, despite the fact they'd known each other only a few hours. But it was more than that. He was fascinated by her.

She was a unique challenge his cat couldn't resist.

Tracing her full mouth with the tip of his tongue he slipped between her lips and tasted her decadent sweetness. The breath was ripped from his body. She tasted of summer lilacs with the tart edge of lemon.

A tantalizing combination that was as enticing as the female who trembled in his arms.

His kiss deepened and Indy lifted her hands to press them against his chest. Shit. Was she about to pull away? A growl rumbled in Angel's chest.

She was as aroused as he was. He could smell her desire. She might want to kick him in the nuts, but she still wanted him.

Then, without warning, she was melting into his arms.

Holy. Crap.

Pleasure blistered through him. It was a kiss. Just a kiss. He'd enjoyed thousands of them. But never had his entire body clenched with a hunger that nearly sent him to his knees. And certainly, his cat had never responded with such a fierce desire to claim a female.

"You're not the only one who's lost their mind," she muttered.

"Good." He caught her lower lip between his teeth. "Sanity is highly overrated."

Her fingers grasped the soft folds of his sweater as Angel slid his hands beneath her jacket and up the curve of her spine. She was so delicate. So astonishingly tiny in his hands. It was easy to forget her fragility when she was in full battle-mode.

Now he reminded himself to use gentle care as he smoothed his hands down to her hips. With a muttered curse he skimmed light kisses over her cheek before he stroked the shell of her ear with his tongue.

She shivered beneath his touch and he felt that strange searing heat blast through him. A heat that was echoed in the beast prowling just below his skin.

65

He wanted to press her against the wall and wrap her legs around his waist. Or toss her on the floor and spread her beneath him. To part her thighs and lick the cream that was already gathering. To thrust himself into her until they were both exhausted and sated.

Instead he stiffened as he caught an unmistakable scent of Pantera swiftly approaching.

No, not now, he silently pleaded, well aware that he'd blown his opportunity to warn Indy that his brothers were on their way.

And now it was too late.

There was the sound of pounding footsteps before the door was smashed open and Bayon stepped into the room, one golden brow flicking upward as a devilish smile curved his lips.

At the same time Indy yanked out of his arms, her face flushed with fury. And worse, her eyes dark with a sense of utter betrayal.

"You bastard," she husked.

CHAPTER 5

Indy was livid.

Not mad. Not angry. Not furious.

Livid.

She'd made mistakes in her past. She was impetuous, passionate, and too eager to listen to her heart, not her head. Which meant she often found herself in situations she later regretted.

But never, ever had she allowed a man to screw with her head to the point that a dozen Pantera Hunters had been able to sneak up on her.

Dammit. She was supposed to be protecting her people. They depended on her.

Instead she'd been melting in Angel's arms, completely seduced by his kisses.

Snarling out every curse word she'd learned over the past thirty years, Indy yanked at the handcuffs that were attached to the wooden headboard.

She didn't know how she ended up in the wide bed. Only seconds after the door had crashed in she'd felt a pinprick of pain as a dart had penetrated the skin of her neck. She'd had time to accept the irony of the fact she'd been tranqed before she was tumbling into

67

Angel's arms, the blackness sucking her under.

She'd awoken nearly an hour ago to find herself cuffed to the bed. In bewilderment she'd studied the wooden furniture that looked handcrafted, and a patchwork quilt that covered her body that'd been stripped down to her muscle shirt and jeans.

There was an air of homey warmth that was only emphasized as she glanced out the window to glimpse the thick foliage and clumps of cypress trees that provided a dense shade the late afternoon sunlight was unable to penetrate.

She was in the bayou.

Or more specifically…she was in the Wildlands.

There was the sound of approaching footsteps before the door was pushed open. Indy tensed. Even from a distance she could recognize the familiar scent.

Angel.

The sight of him only made her more livid. Livider?

Not just because he'd tricked her and used her vulnerable desires against her. She was willing to fight dirty when necessary. But because the mere sight of him moving toward the bed was making her heart pound and her blood heat with arousal.

Helplessly her gaze clung to his impossibly handsome features and the white-gold hair that was spiked as if he'd been running his fingers through it. He'd showered and changed into a pair of charcoal gray slacks and a crisp white shirt that should have lessened the impact of his raw, fiercely disturbing presence.

But it didn't.

Instead, she'd never been more aware of the cat that lurked just below the surface.

Her stomach quivered as he settled on the edge of the bed, his gaze studying her with dark intensity.

"Bastard," she ground out, hoping like hell he assumed her flushed cheeks were due to fury, not seething lust.

He grimaced. "This isn't how I wanted it to be," he murmured in soft tones.

"Ha." She narrowed her eyes, her expression accusing. "Don't tell me you're not enjoying your revenge?"

A hint of gold flared through his eyes. "I'll admit I have a few fantasies that include you in handcuffs," he admitted, his gaze sweeping down her body. "But you were naked and moaning my name in pleasure."

Oh...hell. Now the image was blasted in her brain.

"Where am I?"

"The Wildlands." He confirmed her suspicion. "This cabin belonged to my parents."

He had her locked in his family home? That seemed...odd.

"What are you going to do to me?"

He frowned, as if disturbed by her question. "No one here means you harm, Indy." Reaching into his pocket, he pulled out a key and swiftly unlocked the cuffs. "See?"

She barely waited for her the cuffs to fall away before she was surging onto her knees and slamming her fist into his shoulder.

"Take that, you bastard," she snapped.

His brows snapped together, his hand reaching to grasp her wrist. Not to halt her from hitting him again—even with her super-strength it'd felt like she'd hit a cement wall—but to study her fingers as if concerned she'd injured herself.

"What was that for?" he growled.

"Kissing me."

He arched a brow. Was that amusement glinting in his eyes?

Arrgh.

"Do you slug every male who kisses you?" he asked.

"Only ones who use sex to keep me distracted so his friends can sneak up on me."

He held her furious glare, lifting her fingers to press them against his lips.

"We both know that's not why I kissed you, Indy," he said in low tones.

"No?"

"Do you want the truth?" She could glimpse his cat deep in his eyes, the beast studying her with the intensity of a predator on the verge of consuming its prey. "Once I say it, I can't take it back."

The world came to a halt. Not just a halt, but a screeching halt.

Was he implying…

Something close to panic had her abruptly changing the subject.

"Where are the others?"

He smiled with wry resignation before he gave her fingers another lingering kiss.

"With the Healers."

A sizzle of raw arousal scalded her at his light caress, but Indy grimly refused to be distracted.

"Why?" she demanded, her voice hard with suspicion. "Were they hurt?"

He made a sound of annoyance, as if offended by her question.

"Of course not. We wanted to run some tests."

Indy was instantly outraged, trying to tug her hand free so she could give him another slug.

"Damn you."

Rolling his eyes, he leaned to the side and grabbed a wooden figurine.

"Here." He pressed the carving into her hand and curled her fingers around it. "If you're going to hit me then use this."

She glanced down in confusion. "Why?"

"I don't want you to hurt your hand."

Well, damn.

Her anger floundered as she heaved a deep sigh. Then, lifting her head, she met his steady gaze.

"I told you what happened to them in New York," she breathed. "How could you put them through that again?"

He cupped her cheek in his palm, running his thumb down the stubborn line of her jaw.

"Absolutely nothing is being done to them without their full consent," he assured her.

Indy wasn't impressed. These Pantera hadn't been there when she'd found little Caleb strapped to his bed and so filthy she could barely see his skin. Or Nadia who was so terrified she hadn't spoken for nearly a year. Or little Willa who'd been trapped in a cage…

"Why can't you leave them alone? They've been through enough."

His thumb traced the curve of her lower lip. "Indy, we need to make sure they don't have any damage from the experiments they were forced to endure."

She stilled. Okay. Maybe it was a good thing the Healers could make sure they were all right. But that didn't mean for a second she believed that was the only reason they were in the Wildlands.

"And that's all?" she prodded.

He hesitated, as if choosing his words with care. No doubt a good thing. Indy was eager to use any excuse to try and make him the enemy.

How else was she going to resist the unnerving need to crawl into his lap and never leave?

"I'll admit that we hope to discover what Locke and his men were trying to achieve," he finally admitted.

"What does it matter?"

His fingers lightly skimmed downward, lingering on the pulse that pounded at the base of her throat.

"Once we know the end-game it might help us track down the people responsible."

She gave a slow nod. In the beginning she'd considered it her personal mission to find the men who'd created the labs and destroy them. Even if it cost her life, she was going to rid the world of the bastards.

Experience, however, had taught her that the organization was way too large, and too well-funded for her to tackle alone.

Having the Pantera out for blood was something she could actually cheer. As long as they didn't use her people to gain their revenge.

"You'll let them leave whenever they want?" she pressed.

His fingers moved down her shoulder, his expression distracted.

"As long as they promise not to reveal our weakness to malachite."

Hmm. That seemed way too easy. "No tricks?"

"No tricks." His exploring fingers continued down her arm, his lips curling in satisfaction as a tremor shook her body. "But I'm not so sure they're going to want to leave."

She sucked in a shuddering breath, barely capable of concentrating on his words as he retraced a path back up her arm.

His skin was so hot. And his musky scent was teasing at her senses, intoxicating her with a hunger that was spiraling out of control.

"Why wouldn't they want to leave?" she managed to ask.

Without warning he was shoving himself upright and tugging her off the bed.

"Come here."

She allowed herself to be led to the window, struggling to keep her balance. Her legs weren't entirely stable after lying on the bed for hours.

Reaching the window, Angel pointed toward the large black puma with pale green eyes that was stretched out in a patch of sunlight while it watched the small golden cub awkwardly pouncing at a stray leaf.

Her eyes widened in fascination. She'd never actually seen a Pantera shifted into their animal form. It was...

"Astonishing," she breathed.

His hand brushed down the curve of her back. "Look closer."

With a confused frown her gaze studied the magnificent older puma before returning to the smaller cat. Slowly she realized there was something familiar about the cub. It wasn't anything she could see with her eyes. It was more a feeling.

At last she gave a low cry of shock. "Oh my god. Willa."

"Yes." There was an edge of anger in the clipped word. "She was sick because she wasn't able to shift until she was in the Wildlands."

Joy spread through Indy as she watched the cub leap forward, attacking the larger puma's tail. There was no mistaking the health and happiness that had been decidedly absent when Willa was in her human form.

"She's beautiful, but..." Indy gave a shake of her head, turning to meet Angel's dark gaze. "I don't understand. She was human."

"It's impossible to know for sure," he admitted, his features tight with frustration. His concern for Willa was palpable. "Which makes it all the more imperative that we discover where they've relocated so we can get our hands on the medical files."

Unexpectedly, something eased deep inside her.

She'd demanded a lot of herself over the years. Not only by caring for people she'd claimed as her own, but for constantly trying to find ways of releasing even more victims from the labs.

She hadn't known how heavy the burden was until Angel had come along and forced her to accept his help.

Still, along with the relief was an unmistakable sense of bittersweet sadness. It felt as if a chapter in her life was closing before she'd prepared herself to say goodbye.

"Are the others okay?" she asked.

His features softened with a fond amusement. "Nadia has come out of her shell, asking a thousand questions of my staff."

"I suspected she had healing powers."

"She does," Angel assured her. "Tarin is hovering protectively at her side while Caleb has attached himself to Parish, the leader of our Hunters."

"You're a fast worker," she murmured.

"Would you prefer they were still hiding in a building that was one stiff breeze from total destruction?"

She gave an instant shake of her head. "No. Of course not."

His thumb slid beneath her chin, tilting back her pale face to meet his searching gaze.

"What's wrong?"

"I've started getting used to having them around," she admitted with a wry smile.

Slowly he lowered his head, brushing her lips with an achingly tender kiss.

"You had a small family and now you have a much larger family," he told her.

Her breath tangled in her throat. There was something dangerously tempting in his soft words.

With an abrupt movement she stepped back. "What do you want from me?"

A wicked heat flared through his eyes, his potent musk clouding her mind.

"I need you to share everything you know with Raphael," he said, prowling forward.

Her mouth went dry, a layer of sweat coating her skin. It was hot. So deliciously, enticingly hot.

"Fine," she managed to force past her stiff lips. "But first…"

With liquid grace, Angel had her scooped off her feet and carried back to the bed.

"Wait," she breathed, shocked by the speed of her intense arousal.

"No more waiting," he growled, settling her in the center of the mattress. Before she could move, he was leaning over her, a blatant need etched onto his beautiful face. "My cat has hungered for your taste since the first second you crossed my path."

Indy should have been terrified. There was no mistaking the predator that lurked in his eyes.

Instead, she felt as if a spell was being woven around her. And maybe it was. That would explain why the air suddenly felt as if it was vibrating with the passion exploding between them. And why her body was growing wet with anticipation.

"Angel?"

His gaze scanned her flushed face, lingering on the lush curve of her mouth before it skimmed down her slender body.

"I always forget how tiny you are," he admitted with a rueful smile.

She struggled to breathe at the sight of the raw desire that rippled over his face.

"I'm not small, I'm compact," she husked.

His lips twitched as his gaze lowered to her breasts that were clearly outlined by the tight muscle shirt.

"You're perfect," he breathed.

"The others will be looking for me," she rasped, trying to cling to sanity.

A wasted effort as his hand slid along her throat, seemingly fascinated by the feel of her skin.

"I warned them that I intended to keep you handcuffed to my bed until you admitted you're mine."

Her eyes widened in disbelief. "You told them I was handcuffed to your bed?"

He lowered his head, brushing his lips over her temple. "Don't worry. They're all very happy for you."

He planted kisses over her cheek, lingering at the edge of her mouth.

"Liar," she breathed even as her heart thundered in her chest. Holy crap. Her entire body was on fire. Her stomach clenched with desire, and her clit tingled with eager impatience.

And even more astonishing was the realization that she no longer wanted to fight this terrible desire.

Indy was a realist at heart. She'd accepted that there was no small cottage and picket fence in her future. Not when she'd sworn revenge on her enemies.

Now suddenly Angel was turning everything upside down.

As if sensing her inner turmoil, Angel nibbled at the lobe of her ear, his hands lightly running down her arms.

"They want you to be happy," he whispered.

"And they think handcuffs are going to make me happy?"

"No, they think I am."

His gaze remained locked on her face as he moved to stretch next to her, his chiseled features taut with need.

Her body melted as he wrapped her in his arms, her hands eagerly tugging open the buttons of his shirt to explore the heated silk of his skin.

"Christ, Indy," he breathed. "If you only knew how desperately I've wanted to feel your hands explore me."

She shivered as he impatiently tugged the muscle shirt out of her jeans so his fingers could slide beneath the thin material. At the same time his lips traced the line of her jaw before brushing lightly over her mouth.

"You should be locked away for the safety of all women, Dr. Savary."

"I'd gladly be locked away as long as you're with me, sweet Indy."

The fantasy of having this male handcuffed to the bed so she could keep him entirely to herself raced through her mind as his mouth closed over hers in a searching kiss. Insane? Hell, yeah. But tempting. The cuffs were just inches away and...

She allowed her brief flare of madness to melt away. Desire, as sweet and warm as the finest liqueur, flowed through her body and her fingers bit deep into his shoulders.

Parting her lips, she returned his kiss with unrestrained desire, a low moan lodging in her throat as he threaded his fingers through her hair.

His touch was so gentle—almost reverent as he smoothed the spiky strands from her face. It was an enticing contrast to the pulsing hardness of the male body pressed against her.

She could taste his need on her lips, but there was no haste in his seduction.

His mouth moved along the side of her face, pausing to nip the lobe of her ear before he buried his face in the curve of her neck. He breathed deeply of her scent.

Indy made a small sound of contentment. She'd expected the blazing heat and intense passion that sizzled between them, but she hadn't expected the sense of being...treasured. It was oddly more unnerving than the scorching pleasure of his mouth as it returned to hers.

With a smooth motion his hands gripped the neckline of her shirt, ripping it in two with shocking ease. Indy blinked in surprise, but before she could protest, his hands were cupping her breasts, his thumbs teasing the tight buds of her nipples.

Oh...yes. That's exactly what she wanted. She arched her back in encouragement.

"Yes," he muttered at her wanton response, his hands lowering to swiftly tug off the rest of her clothing.

Within seconds she was completely naked.

Instinctively her hand reached for the quilt. She'd

always been self-conscious of her boyish lack of curves. Slender was one thing. Skinny…yeah, not so attractive. Angel, however, grabbed her wrist, lifting her fingers to press them against his mouth.

"Please, don't hide from me," he rasped, his eyes glowing with a golden fire. "You're so beautiful."

Indy sucked in a deep breath. Beneath his fierce gaze she felt beautiful.

Releasing a soft groan, Angel was hastily wrenching off his clothes, his movements oddly jerky as he revealed the sculpted perfection of his chest that tapered to a lean waist. His legs were long, with heavy muscles, and his erection…

The air was wrenched from her lungs at the sight of the thick cock that curled toward the flat plane of his stomach, the heavy length fully aroused.

He was truly spectacular.

Her hand reached to stroke him, but with a muttered curse he was grabbing her wrists and yanking her arms over her head.

"Hey…"

Her protest was cut short as he lowered his head and kissed her with a growing urgency.

Still holding her arms pinned to the bed he allowed his mouth to begin to explore her body with frustrating leisure. He lingered at the base of her throat, planting teasing kisses over the line of her collarbone and then, at last, he found the straining tip of her breast.

Indy released a shaky sigh, her toes curling as pleasure blistered through her. Good god. She'd enjoyed a few one-night stands. Why not? She was a young, healthy woman with needs. But nothing had prepared her for the wicked excitement his touch sent jolting through her.

The heat of his lips as they sucked her, the rough caress of his tongue, and even the less-than-gentle bite of his teeth. It was all enough to make her arch upward in a shuddering bliss.

"This is just the beginning, Indy," he murmured against her skin. "You belong to me."

Indy barely heard his harsh words. She was lost in a daze of sensual need.

There could surely be nothing better than this?

He proved her wrong as his hands loosened their grip on her arms and skimmed down the planes of her body. Wherever they traveled they left behind a buzz of electric sensations, like tiny sparklers flaring over her skin.

Her breath caught in surprise as his hands reached her legs and jerked them apart.

"I can smell your sweet honey," he muttered, his mouth moving to tease the hollow between her breasts. "I need to taste it."

Ever so slowly he kissed his way down her body, stopping to inspect the small heart tattooed on her hipbone.

"Angel?" she murmured in confusion.

"You were injured," he growled.

She blinked in surprise. How did he know the heart covered one of the cigarette burns that'd been left by her mother?

"It's nothing," she assured him.

A low growl rumbled in his chest. "Never again, Indy," he swore softly. "No one will ever hurt you again."

Warmth flooded through her at his fierce promise, but before she could respond, Angel returned to determined exploration of her body.

Indy clenched the blanket beneath her as the roaming lips at last found her moist center, his tongue stroking between the tender folds.

"Yes," she gasped.

His head lifted to study her with eyes that held a very cat-like satisfaction.

"You smell like wildflowers and taste like honey."

Indy blushed as he held her gaze. She was an idiot, but Angel made her feel like a giddy teenager. It was intoxicating.

Slowly he lowered his head, his tongue creating all sorts of sinful havoc as he continued to stroke and tease her. Her head fell back against the pillow as tension clutched her body.

She was close.

"Now, Angel," she rasped, unwilling to climax before she felt him buried deep inside her.

Heat prickled in the air as he surged up her body, his mouth claiming her parted lips as he settled between her thighs. Indy lifted her arms, shoving her fingers into the soft silk of his hair.

She made a sound of pleasure as she felt the brush of his hard cock press against her entrance.

At last...

She had time to grasp his shoulders before he was surging into her dampness with a ruthless shove.

Lost in the savage pleasure, Indy dug her nails into his back and gave a muffled gasp. He was large enough to stretch her to the edge of pain, but damn, nothing had ever felt so good.

Angel moaned, his hands skimming down to grasp her hips, angling her up to receive his deepening thrusts.

"I thought this could never happen to me," he said in husky tones, burying his face in the curve of her neck.

Her legs wrapped around his waist, her hips lifting to meet each surge of his cock.

Bliss. Sheer bliss.

"What couldn't happen?" she managed to whisper.

"You." He lightly kissed her lips before pulling back to regard her with a somber expression. "Us."

"Why?"

Angel kept his gaze locked on hers as he increased the pace, the heady scent of his musk clinging to her skin.

"My life was supposed to be dedicated to duty." He lowered his head to nuzzle at her throat. "A mate was never part of the equation."

Indy dug her nails into his shoulders as her breaths came in short gasps, the pleasure coalescing into a burst of shocking waves.

Above her, Angel's features sharpened as he gave one last forceful thrust and then, with a wrenching groan, he collapsed on top of her.

In a rather dazed wonderment Indy held onto him with weak arms.

Mate.

Good. God.

CHAPTER 6

Angel kept his arms locked tight around Indy as they snuggled in the center of the bed.

His death grip had more than one purpose. Number one was the simple pleasure in feeling this female pressed against his body. He was confident this was as close to paradise as he'd ever been. And number two was ensuring she didn't run from him in horror.

His lips pressed to her temple as his gaze skimmed down her naked body to the curve of her hip where the silvery claw marks glistened in the late afternoon sunlight.

Savage satisfaction raced through him along with a belated stab of guilt.

"Are you okay?" he demanded.

She tilted her head back, her cheeks still flushed and her eyes smoldering with a remembered pleasure.

"I'm tougher than I look," she said.

Angel couldn't argue. For such a tiny thing she had the heart and courage of a warrior. She was also an intensely independent woman.

Which was what troubled him.

"I mean…" His fingers drifted down her body to the shallow claw marks. "Are you freaking out at the thought of being my mate?"

Her lips twisted with wry amusement. "Would it change anything if I did?"

"No," he admitted without hesitation. "It's far too late."

Belatedly glancing to where his fingers traced the silvery lines on her hip, she made a sound of surprise.

"What's that?"

He tried to hide his smug smile. "My mark."

"Mark?" She tilted back her head to study him in confusion.

His hand cupped her hip in blatant possession. He should no doubt have resisted the urge to slice his claws through her flesh as he'd felt her climax gripping his cock, but the overpowering instinct had simply taken over before he could rationally consider the consequences.

"My claim as your mate."

"Yeesh," she muttered. "Couldn't you have just bought me a diamond ring?"

Relief jolted through him at her teasing tone. She had every right to be annoyed. He was a Pantera, which meant he'd known without a doubt they were meant to be together. His cat had chosen her as his mate. End of story.

But she was human.

Which meant her emotions could be far more murky.

But there was no mistaking the warm, profound contentment that settled on her pale face.

"I would buy you a hundred rings if I thought they would make you happy, but I have a feeling you would prefer a new dagger," he told her, glancing toward the chair near the door where he'd left her leather jacket.

He'd found two daggers and a dart gun filled with malachite in various pockets.

Her fingers drew aimless patterns over his chest, the light caress sending a raging inferno through him. He shuddered. He'd heard males say that nothing could compare to being intimate with a true mate, but he'd assumed they were exaggerating.

Now he realized their words hadn't even begun to capture the extraordinary sensations of feeling Indy's hands stroking over his skin.

"A girl has to protect herself," she teased.

His possessive urge to guard and care for the female he had claimed as his own roared through him.

"No more," he growled. "Now that's my job."

Instantly she stiffened, her hands pressing against his chest."

"Hold on."

Realizing his mistake, Angel dipped his head down to press a swift kiss to her lips.

"I know, you're a warrior," he assured her. Indy would be miserable if he tried to wrap her in a protective bubble. She'd already been held hostage by Locke. He wasn't going to use their mating to cage her. "I will never try to make you less, Indy, but from now on we work as a team."

He felt her tension ease, her fingers resuming their distracting exploration over his chest and down to his stomach.

"You said you never expected to mate," she abruptly said. "It can't just be because of your dedication to duty."

He swallowed a groan. How the hell was he supposed to think when her hand was just an inch from his straining cock?

"My father died in an accident when I was just a cub," he managed to mutter, his hand cupping her ass to press her against the hard thrust of his erection. "I was raised by my mother."

He scented the sweet honey of her arousal, but she studied him with blatant curiosity.

"You were close to your mother?"

A familiar pain clenched his heart, but this time it was tempered by the newfound emotions the female in his arms had stirred to life.

He would always mourn the loss of his parents, but Indy had helped to fill the hole in his heart.

"Yes." He brushed his lips over the top of her head, deeply regretting that Indy's mother had been a worthless bitch. Thankfully Indy now had a family who would love her without question. "Then the Wildlands started to fade and she was infected with a rare Pantera disease."

She frowned in confusion. "I thought you were immune?"

"To human diseases, but there have been a few Pantera that were vulnerable to the evil that the disciples of Shakpi used to infect our homelands."

"Oh." Clearly aware of the goddess who'd done her best to destroy the Pantera, Indy leaned forward to press a soft kiss just below his ear. "I'm sorry. It must have been very painful."

"It was. That's when I swore I would devote my life to my responsibility as a Healer."

"And now?"

His lips skimmed over her brow and down the length of her nose. "Now I realize that I need more than duty. I need you." Placing a lingering kiss on her lips, he pulled back to regard her with a gaze of pure longing. "Will you stay with me and be my mate, Indy?"

She didn't make him wait.

"Yes, Angel," she breathed. "I'll be your mate."

He buried his face in the curve of her neck, breathing deep of her scent of wildflowers.

"Thank the Goddess."

"But…"

He growled, giving her skin a light nip before he lifting his head to study her with a wry smile.

"Why did I know there was going to be a but?"

"I can't stop my mission until every lab has been found and destroyed," she said, her expression settling into stubborn lines.

"I know," he said. And he did. This woman had been held captive, tortured, and experimented on. The only way she would be able to make sense of her life was to bring an end to the bastards who'd treated her as an animal. "As long as you accept that you don't have to be Wonder Woman anymore."

She snorted, a wicked smile teasing at her lips. "I would never fill out Wonder Woman's outfit."

His gaze lowered to the rounded globes of her breasts that were tipped with rosy nipples. His mouth instantly watered.

He hadn't devoted nearly enough time tasting those tempting buds.

"You're perfect. You're beautiful and courageous and loyal and…" His words trailed away with a husky groan as her fingers at last closed around his aching cock.

"And?" she teased, scattering kisses over his chest.

"Mine," he rasped, grasping her leg to tug it over his hip, leaving her exposed for his cock to slide into her with one steady thrust.

***

Stanton polished off the last of the gumbo he'd sent the guard to pick up from Chelsea's favorite restaurant. In the back of his mind he knew it was a mistake to prolong this encounter. Not only because it made the inevitable parting even more painful, but because every minute he was in her presence he risked exposing her to his master.

But when had he ever allowed logic and common sense to clutter his mind when it came to this woman?

It was at last Chelsea who brought an end to his afternoon of insanity.

Collecting their plates, she moved to place them in the sink before turning to watch as he rose from the table.

"You haven't told me why you're here."

He allowed his gaze to drink in the beauty of her fiery curls surrounding the perfect oval of her face. A face only made more beautiful by the scars that proved she was a survivor.

"New Orleans has become too dangerous to continue our research here," he said, grimacing at the enormous loss of property they'd suffered over the past week. In total he'd been forced to burn four labs and two homes.

This one would be next.

Chelsea arched a brow. "You're afraid the Pantera might at last hunt you down and rip out your heart?"

Stanton shrugged. He wasn't stupid. He knew the beast-men would shred him to tiny, bloody pieces if they ever managed to get their hands on him. Thankfully, the Pantera had been happy to remain hidden in their swamps so long he'd been able to create several layers of security around his various businesses, including emergency evacuation plans.

Still, the fact that they now had him on their radar meant he could no longer take unnecessary risks.

"They have become a..." He searched for the appropriate word. "Complication."

Chelsea gave a sharp laugh. Unlike Stanton, she'd developed an inability to dismiss the Pantera as mere test subjects. And that, of course, had been her problem.

Once she saw them as people with feelings and dreams instead of just creatures, she'd been unable to continue with her research.

"A very dangerous complication," Chelsea taunted.

"They won't be able to stop us," Stanton said with genuine confidence. The animals were dangerous, but they weren't nearly as tech savvy as he was. "But for now we've transferred our patients to our other labs."

She frowned. "I thought your master was convinced that Hiss would be the answer to all his troubles."

Stanton hesitated, abruptly knowing where the conversation was headed.

"That's his hope."

"So why do you insist on keeping the other prisoners?"

"The research they provide is invaluable," he said in offhand tones.

She clutched the counter behind her, a profound disappointment making her shoulders droop.

"So it's true," she muttered.

"What?" Stanton tried to bluff.

"You're selling the technology we discovered." She pushed away from the counter, moving to stand directly in front of him. "Locke, how could you?"

He wrenched his gaze from her pained expression, forcing himself to glance out the window where he could see the sky being painted in shades of lavender and pink as dusk began to spread over the city.

He didn't want to try and explain why he'd allowed his master to convince him they should use the experimental drugs they'd created as a way to fund further research.

Not when Chelsea was well aware that nothing could excuse the blatant greed of the older man.

It was one thing to try and discover technology to keep yourself alive. It was another to sell the pain of others for profit.

"I won't be returning to New Orleans." He abruptly changed the conversation.

It was time to walk away.

Before she ended up resenting him even more.

She sucked in a sharp breath. "What happens to me?"

He glanced down at her pale face, memorizing each line and curve. As if her image hadn't already been branded into his brain.

"You're free," he told her.

She seemed to freeze, her eyes wide. "What?"

He grimly ignored the agony that pulsed through him. For once in his miserable life he was going to do the right thing.

Even if it killed him.

"The doors are unlocked and when I leave I'll take the guard with me," he forced himself to say.

She blinked, staring at him with wary hope. "Are you serious?"

"Yes."

"Why?"

Barely aware of what he was doing, he lifted his hand to brush a stray curl behind her ear.

"I realize I was wrong to hold you as my prisoner." His lips twisted, his fingers tingling at the feel of her warm skin. "At first my only concern was ensuring that no one discovered you were still alive. I couldn't bear the thought of you being hurt."

"And then?" she prompted.

He gave a humorless laugh. "Then I kept you here because I hoped we could be together again. Stupid. Holding you captive isn't exactly the way to win your heart."

Regret darkened her eyes, her hand lifting to cup

his face. "I've told you what you needed to do if you want to be together."

She had. All he had to do was betray the man who'd saved his life and turned him into a success.

"I…can't," he ground out.

Her jaw hardened with disappointment. Good lord. Even after all this time she still cared?

The knowledge was oddly painful.

"You'll walk away and leave me?" she husked.

He flinched, deliberately misinterpreting her soft plea.

"You should be safe," he assured her. "The master believes you're dead and as long as you don't deliberately draw attention to yourself there's no reason for him to suspect you're still alive."

She wasn't fooled.

She knew he was avoiding her question.

"This is what you want?" she insisted.

"This is what I want." Framing her face in his hands, Stanton lowered his head to kiss her with a bittersweet longing he felt in his very soul.

"Stay," she whispered against his lips, her hands grasping his shirt in a tight grip.

"Run from here, Chelsea," he urged her, giving her one last kiss before he was pulling away. "Build a new life."

"Locke—"

"Be happy," he pleaded, turning to head out of the kitchen.

Not allowing himself to glance back, he halted only long enough to pay the guard an obscene amount of money to keep his mouth shut before he was climbing into his silver Jag and gunning the engine.

Soon New Orleans would be a speck in his rearview mirror and Chelsea would become a fond memory.

He repeated the words over and over as the city streets were replaced by the tangled greenery of the wetlands, not really surprised when they did nothing to ease the heaviness of his heart.

CHAPTER 7

Indy couldn't deny a stab of surprise when Angel at last led her out of the private cottage into the Wildlands.

Okay, she hadn't expected mud huts and treehouses, but it was all far more civilized than she'd expected.

First they'd headed to the state-of-the-art medical facility where Angel had run a dozen tests on her before she was surrounded by eager Pantera mates who'd pampered her with a hot bath and clean clothes.

Next he'd led her across the open space in the middle of the bayou to reveal the private headquarters of the Suits.

The elegant Colonial-style structure that was painted white with black shutters had an old-world feel to it that was only emphasized by the six fluted columns that held up the second-story balcony.

The inside, however, was buzzing with electric energy and high-tech security systems that would make Homeland Security shit a brick.

Trying to ignore the curious gazes that followed their path through the crowded public rooms, Indy inched closer to Angel. She'd never been surrounded by so many Pantera at once and it was unsettling.

Her nerves weren't eased when they stepped into the private office of a large male with long, golden blond hair and jade green eyes.

The force of two alpha males in the same small place was enough to make her body feel as if it was being pressed between a rock and a very hard place.

The head of the Diplomats rose to his feet at their entrance, blatantly inspecting her as Angel urged her to the center of the room.

"So you're the female who finally captured Angel," he murmured.

Angel gave a sudden laugh, wrapping his arm around Indy's shoulders.

"In more ways than one."

Indy sent her mate a wry smile, recalling how she'd awoken handcuffed to the bed only hours ago.

"Actually, I'm not sure who caught who," she said.

Angel pressed a swift kiss against her temple. "Let's call it a mutual agreement."

Raphael watched them with open satisfaction. "Did you complete your testing?" he asked of Angel.

"Yes," Angel said. "I have a few preliminary results."

Raphael folded his arms over his chest. "And?"

Angel's arm tightened around her shoulder. Only days ago, Indy would have been furious at his possessive touch. Now she relished the knowledge that whatever happened, she would have this glorious male at her side.

"Specific parts of her DNA have been altered," he admitted, the rough growl in his voice pure cat.

Raphael's gaze slid in her direction. "Altered how?"

It was Angel who answered. "I don't know. Which means our enemy has technology way beyond what we understand."

Raphael grimaced. "Perfect." He continued to study her with open concern. "Do you feel okay?"

"I do," Indy told him. "No doubt better than I would if I'd remained a mere human."

"She has increased strength and endurance, and if she's anything like Tarin she's probably immune to most human diseases," Angel added.

Raphael's brows snapped together, his lean body, currently attired in a pair of khakis and a cashmere sweater, rigid with his barely leashed emotions.

"Dammit," he breathed.

"What's wrong?" Angel demanded.

"We're constantly a day late and a dollar short," he snarled, his eyes glowing gold as his hunger for the blood of his enemies prickled in the air. "Tell me what you remember about the labs," he snapped toward Indy.

Angel instantly moved to stand in front of her, his body clenched as he glared at his companion.

"Easy, Raphael," he growled.

Realizing both males were on edge, Indy reached up to run a soothing hand down Angel's back.

"It's okay," she assured her mate, keeping her hand on his lower back as she met Raphael's smoldering gaze. The older male was worried about his people. She better than anyone understood his frustration. "We were divided into different groups. The Pantera were kept in the lower basements. I was never down there so I'm not entirely sure what happened to them."

Raphael abruptly turned to walk across the room that was furnished with a simple but sturdy oak desk and leather chairs, with shelves overflowing with pictures of a pretty dark-haired woman and a newborn child.

"Obviously they had blood and semen taken from them," he said.

"Yes," Angel agreed. "And bone marrow."

Raphael turned back, his expression bleak. "What else?"

Indy didn't know exactly what he wanted to know, so she shared what she assumed was most pertinent.

"There were women used as breeders."

"We've heard about them," Raphael said. "They were using the Haymore Center as a fertility facility."

Indy nodded. "Karen was one, but she was held prisoner in New York. I think there are several other labs scattered around."

"So do I," Raphael swiftly agreed. "Caleb is her son?"

"Yes, plus she has two others who we've been searching for," Indy revealed, hoping her friend didn't mind her sharing the information. If the Pantera went in search of the people responsible for taking them captive, it was possible they might be able to locate her missing sons. "She was never given Pantera blood," she continued. "But she was artificially inseminated with their semen."

Raphael nodded. "Willa must be an offspring created by a breeder."

A growl rumbled deep in Angel's chest. He was already deeply attached to the little girl.

"They've clearly improved their technique over the years," he said.

Raphael nodded, his attention still locked on Indy. "And you?"

"I was a cavy," she revealed without hesitation. She never apologized for being a victim. "We were all test rats used for different experiments."

"You don't know what they wanted from you?" the Pantera male pressed.

"No." Indy shook her head. She'd sensed she was changing, but she'd never had a clue what the end result was supposed to be. "All I know for certain was that they took large vials of blood from me every day."

Raphael's expression tightened, clearly annoyed she couldn't offer the answers he needed. But before he could try to demand more information about what had been done to her, Angel made a low sound of warning.

The older male clenched his jaw, but surprisingly he nodded his head in silent capitulation. Not that he was done questioning her.

"What about the people who were holding you?" He turned his attention to their mutual enemy. Which was just fine with Indy. "Do you know anything about them?"

She wrinkled her nose. She'd spent a lot of time investigating the bastards. Unfortunately, they had the sort of resources that made it almost impossible to penetrate their security.

"The guards were all well trained and well armed," she shared.

Raphael narrowed his eyes. "Military?"

"I would guess they were military trained but after I managed to escape I couldn't find any connection to the government."

"They would make sure they kept it a secret." The male's lips twisted with disgust. "Even animals are supposed to be treated humanely."

"True," Indy murmured. It'd been her first thought as well, but so far she hadn't discovered any link. "From all the information I could dig up, the labs appear to be owned by a private corporation."

"Locke?" Raphael spit the name out like it was a curse.

"He's the one listed on the paperwork." Indy shrugged, searching for the words to express her vague suspicions. "But I sense there's someone else lurking in the shadows."

Indy felt an odd sense of pride as the leader of the Suits gave a brisk nod, accepting her words without question.

She'd half expected to be treated as an outsider, or even as one of the enemy. Instead they'd made her feel as if she was a part of the community.

"Can you lead us to the lab in New York?" Raphael asked.

She grimaced. She'd been expecting the question.

"I can, but it changes every few months," she explained. "I doubt we'll find anything but an abandoned building."

There was a burst of heat as the two males

100

glanced at one another. Clearly they'd hoped she could provide them with a starting place.

The tension in the air was abruptly interrupted as the door was thrust open and a tall stranger with a scarred face and dark hair stepped into the room.

Indy shivered. Christ. If two puma males were enough to make the room seem overly small, then three were enough to make it positively claustrophobic.

Seemingly unaware of thick heat that threatened to choke her, Raphael moved toward the intruder while Angel once again placed an arm around her shoulders, tugging her tight against his side.

"Yes?" Raphael demanded.

The stranger briefly studied Indy before turning his attention to the golden-haired male.

"There's a human female who we caught trying to sneak into the Wildlands," he said, his voice a deep growl.

Raphael swore beneath his breath. "Another reporter?"

The newest Pantera shook his head. "She says her name is Dr. Chelsea Young." A lethal smile curved the male's lips, emphasizing the scars on his lean face. "She claims she can tell us where to find Hiss."

HISS

LAURA WRIGHT

CHAPTER 1

"Hiss?"

"I'm here," he uttered, his eyelids heavy, his heart nearly dead. "Another nightmare?"

She exhaled softly. "They're coming all the time."

Despite the debilitating weakness that lived inside him now, Hiss forced himself from his cot and crawled over to the bars of the cage. Gia's hand was already through the metal, waiting for him. It felt cold. But everything felt cold down here. It was truly where his soul was meant to dwell.

"Tell me," he whispered, desperate for the sound of her voice again. It kept him sane. Though Goddess only knew, he didn't deserve it.

She entwined her fingers with his the way she had every night for the past twenty-two days. He knew it'd been twenty-two because each night before he collapsed, he'd scraped another line into the brick wall of his cage with his fingernail.

"I'm sorry," she breathed.

"You have nothing to be sorry for," he told her. "Ever."

"My weakness, my fear. I hate it. This isn't me, wasn't ever me. I was a water Hunter. Fought an alligator for prey. I hate forcing you to listen to my…"

He gripped her hand so tightly she gasped. Then released it. "Tell me, Gia. Talk to me. Use me. None of us are what we were."

She was quiet for a moment. He hated when she got quiet. It scared the fuck out of him. When a Pantera got quiet down here it meant they'd either been moved or had perished…sometimes in body, sometimes in mind.

"The dream, Gia," he pushed, his voice a harsh whisper. Had to be a whisper. Always. Forget about touching—if they were caught talking, they'd be beaten, and then separated. Hiss had seen it happen more than once. Whoever was running this freak show, torture chamber and laboratory wanted no connections made, no emotions shared.

It's why they'd stolen his mother from him the night he'd first come here. If she truly was his mother. He wasn't certain. More than once he'd wondered if maybe it was a plant, a fabrication to fuck with him, make him feel mentally unstable. Or maybe it was his imagination. Maybe he *was* mentally unstable.

"When they come to get me, I go with them. I don't fight." Gia was talking, telling him her dream. Hiss closed his eyes, let his head fall back against the brick. "I just walk out of my cage and go with them." She tried to move closer to him, tried to thread herself through the metal bars. He felt her shoulder press against his. "It's the same room they always take me to, and I'm docile, you know? I don't fight like I have for the past eight months. I'm hoping it changes how they treat me. I lie down, offer them my arms, wait for the bands—wait for the needles to be shoved into my veins. But they don't do it. They don't want my blood."

His chest tight, Hiss waited for her to continue. He knew where this went. Knew her greatest fear.

"It's not going to happen, Gia."

"You don't know that."

"I'm not going to allow it."

She turned to face him. There were no windows in the Sub. It's what they called the lowest level of wherever they, and at least ten other Pantera, were being held. The Subterranean Level of Hell. Where they were being used. Drained. Infected. Poisoned. Experimented on. Injected. Impregnated. It was pitch black. He couldn't see the outline of her body. But he felt her warm breath on his cheek. He turned to face her too.

"How many times were you bled today?" she asked.

"Only three."

She laughed softly, bitterly. Careful to not let the sound carry. They didn't want to wake up the others. Although it was common for the rest of the Pantera to lie awake.

"We can't even summon our cats," she said. "There's no strength for either one of us to drawn on. We're at their mercy."

"You can draw strength from me, Gia," he said. "Always."

"Oh, Hiss…" She played with his fingers. Reveling

in his touch, his comfort. His valiant words. Not knowing who he was—what he was. The traitor to his kind. A base-level beast. She didn't know because she was from a different sect of Pantera, a secret community set somewhere in Florida, from what he'd been able to gather. She didn't speak of it much. It seemed to pain her to remember. And there was nothing Hiss wanted less than to give her any more pain.

"Tell me something good," she whispered. "Tell me a story. About your Wildlands."

My Wildlands. Had they ever been his? He'd wanted them to be. Back when he'd been a cub, when he had a family, they were. And later when his family had disappeared, when the elders told him—lied to him—about their passing, he'd made some good memories. With friends. All while he plotted against them.

A buzzing started in his head. It came every time he thought about what he'd done. To himself. His family's name. To all the innocent Pantera.

"Hiss?" Gia whispered, her tone desperate.

Yes. I'm here. "You speak of your water often," he began. "But let me tell you of ours. There is a place in the bayou where the water is so warm and so fragrant it lulls you to sleep. It changes you from cat to male at whim. And you let it because you trust it. I would swim for hours in it, floating among the Dyesse lilies, so calm, so peaceful."

"What are those? The Dyesse lilies?"

"They're these large, white water lilies. They turn purple when they bloom. And they make our moon purple, too."

"Really?" she exclaimed softly, and he could almost hear her smile. "Oh, how beautiful. I'd love to see that."

His gut ached. Not from the hunger that constantly plagued him. But from the knowledge that he would never be able to take her there. He wasn't welcome. And odds were that he wouldn't be leaving the Sub alive anyway.

"The lilies have this incredible scent," he continued. "We believe…" *We.* His nostrils flared. "They have magical properties that create absolute happiness within us, and a kind of sensual euphoria."

"Oh."

The word came out breathy, warm, and his lips twitched ever so slightly.

"Did you meet your females there?" she asked tentatively. "In the pool? Among the lilies? Under that purple moon?"

"I have no female, Gia." *I deserve no female.* "Where you're from, did you leave a male behind?" It was something he'd wanted to ask the first night they'd 'met.' The night she'd been drained of blood so badly, she was having trouble breathing and couldn't move off the floor. He'd forced his arm through the bar to hold her hand. He'd stayed like that until dawn, everything from his shoulder down numb.

"Yes, I have a male," she said.

Rarely did the cat inside Hiss attempt to emerge. After all, he was out of the Wildlands, devoid of magic. It wasn't possible for his puma to be released. But hearing that Gia had been claimed by another had the beast clawing at the walls of his chest.

109

HISS
LAURA WRIGHT

"His name?" Hiss asked in a harsh whisper. He wasn't sure why he wanted to know it—why he needed to know it.

"I call him Grandfather."

It took only a moment to register, but when it did he felt her smile in the dark.

"Gia…" he said, almost pained.

"Keep talking," she urged, her thumb moving over his palm in small circles. "Tell me more about the lilies and the pools, and your cat, and the Wildlands. Paint me a picture, Hiss. Just until I fall asleep."

He would. Then he would have to ease his hand from hers and return to his cot. Having the guards find them locked together in the morning would surely be their demise.

Not that he cared about himself. He was destined for death, the certain path of a Pantera traitor. But not Gia. He was going to make sure she lived…and found a way out of here…found a way home if it was the last thing he ever did.

"When I was a young cat," he began, "I foolishly tried to consume one of those lilies."

"Oh no," she whispered, laughing softly.

"Quiet now, female," he ordered gently. "Close your eyes. Let me help you sleep."

***

Gia woke, as she often did, to the flicker of fluorescent lights and the sounds of cage doors groaning open and Pantera being hauled out. The guards always started on Side A. Taking two at a time, while Side B got fed. It had been that way every morning since she'd arrived nearly eight months ago.

Since she was snatched off the streets of Miami after visiting her cousin.

Her eyes slid to the cage beside her. He was there, standing in the very center, as he always was, waiting. No matter how weary, how blood-drained he was, he fought them. Sometimes it seemed there was more blood on the floor of his cage than left in his body. Maybe that was why he did it.

Her gaze moved over him, as curious as she was coveting. He was very tall, and though he hadn't had much to eat since he'd come to the Sub, he retained most of his thick muscle. His head was skull shaved most days now, but she knew his hair was thick and black. His face was starkly, brutally handsome, and she often wondered what it looked like when he smiled.

He was nude. The only Pantera who was. She'd seen why a few days after he'd come. Every time he fought the guards, the standard gray sweatpants all the males wore would either get ripped up or bloody or both. Finally, they stopped giving them to him.

He didn't seem to care.

Gia did though. There were female guards, and a few male guards, who stopped to taunt him, stare at his incredible form, threaten him with more than just looking. Though she had no right to claim him in her mind, he was her male. He'd saved her from losing what had been left of her mind. He gave her hope that maybe, just maybe, she would see her Wetlands again.

He glanced her way then and though he didn't smile, never smiled, she felt the deep longing—the need to connect—in his stark gray gaze. He was such a tortured male. In deep pain. And she knew it hadn't just come from being here. He'd been that way when he arrived.

"Hungry, kitty cats?" The male guard called Dax who serviced their side of the Sub moved down the row with a stack of bowls. Though choked full of supplements, the food was barely palatable. But it was all there was.

After sliding Hiss his bowl, Dax walked straight past Gia without even glancing her way. Her stomach growled, then rolled.

"Wait," she called out, despising how desperate she sounded. "I didn't get mine."

Dax looked over his shoulder at her, his watery blue eyes moving from her face down her body. "Oh, you'll get yours, sweetheart."

She shivered in the overlarge black smock that came to just above the knee. It wasn't all that alluring, but to socially awkward, oversexed guards it might as well be lingerie.

"Why is she not being fed?" Hiss demanded.

Gia turned and gave him a shake of the head. *Don't.*

He ignored her. He was at the front of his cage, thick fingers wrapped around the bars. "If you're short a bowl," he ground out, "she can have mine."

The guard had finished passing out bowls now, and was making his way back to Gia's cage. He took out his keys.

"You're coming with me, sweet thing," he said, strangely not using her lab name, Ca35.

"Why?" she asked, her insides starting to hum with anxiety. They never took her blood this early.

"Save your questions for the doc," he said. "Now, are you going to be a nice kitten? Or does Dax have to use the cuffs on you?"

He looked like he really wanted her to act up. He was such a disgusting prick. She glanced over at Hiss. He was at the bars of her cage now, looking as feral and as close to a puma as she'd ever seen him. Her heart lurched. It was glorious. She wished she could see him in his cat form.

A cold, clammy hand wrapped around her wrist. Dax was in her cage, behind her. He shoved her toward the door.

"Don't touch her," Hiss snarled, banging on the bars. "Don't you fucking touch her."

"It's okay," she called back as Dax laughed. "I'll be okay."

But as she was being led away, toward the elevators, Hiss's feral cries continued. They followed her. She could hear him, slamming himself against the bars. *Stop*, she wanted to scream. *You need your strength too*. But he knew, as she knew, that this was no cavy run.

She watched as Dax hit the third button. They always went to two. Never higher than that. Her heart slammed against her ribs.

"Someone's in heat over you, sweet thing," Dax said when the elevator door closed. "Can't say I blame him."

Gia refused to look at him. He made her sick to her stomach.

"Why do you act like you're better than any of us, sweet thing? Us guards. Who take care of you. Feed you." He took a step toward her. "You're not."

He took another step. "Get away from me," she warned.

He laughed, his crooked teeth on full display. "If I wanted to, I could keep you in here all day." He came at her now, and didn't stop until she was pressed against the metal wall. Then he leaned in, near her ear. "On your back. Legs spread. I love Pantera pussy. So much sweeter than the human bitches I have to make due with."

Gia tried not to breathe him in. If this piece of human trash ever ventured into the Everglades, to her Wetlands, her cat would rip his fucking throat out and toss it to the gators.

But her cat was inside her, pacing furiously in a cage of its own.

The guard licked the shell of her ear. "And then you'll return the favor. I may not be as hung as those males you're used to, but I can make the back of your throat burn."

"Oh, me too," she growled, then without thinking, brought her knee up between his legs. Hard. "And a few other parts as well," she ground out.

He dropped back instantly. Then doubled over, wheezing. His head came up just an inch, and his eyes were wide and tear-filled as he stared at her—like he couldn't believe what she'd done.

Gia was having a hard time believing it too. Right now the bastard couldn't get any air in, but what happened when he *was* breathing right again? Forget cuffs, he'd do something ten times more vile to her as payback. She knew it.

The elevator door opened on three, and without even a look in his direction, she scrambled out and took off down a hallway. It reminded her of the hospital ward in Miami, and was deserted, thank Goddess. But only that first one. The minute she turned the corner, she heard voices and backed the hell up. She hid behind an opened door, making herself as small as possible. Then tried to quiet her breathing. What was on the third floor? She knew some of what happened in this building. Blood draws, injections, transplants…but her ultimate fear was the rumors of forced pregnancy.

She would never allow her body to be used that way.

She'd rather die.

A woman passed by the door where she was hidden. A nurse, holding the hands of two children. They looked to be around five or six. Her insides clenched and bile rose in her throat. Were they experimenting on children?

"Br17 in surgery," a male said on the other side of the door. "The pregnancy didn't take. Why do we keep bothering with these human women? A few can handle the rigors of a puma gestational period, but most cannot."

"He wants the human/Pantera DNA," a female explained. "And whatever our gracious benefactor wants, he gets."

The man snorted.

"We have a puma female coming up this

morning," the woman said. "The doctor will impregnate her with human sperm."

"And if it doesn't take?"

"The first few times are always difficult. Like oil and water. But strangely, the female adapts." She sighed. "And if AI doesn't work, we can try breeding naturally."

"The guards would be the first to volunteer," the male tossed in with thread of disgust. "Me? I wouldn't touch one of those animals for all the money in the world. Dax or Peter are just aching for it. Thought we might have to let them go over all the drooling they do. But maybe not. Maybe they serve a bigger purpose here."

Breathing heavy, Gia fought for control over her mind. A thousand thoughts were whirring around like a cyclone. Truly, she couldn't believe what she was hearing. Didn't want to believe it. Goddess, it was ten times worse than any of the nightmares she'd had in her cage. They were going to use her for breeding. And keep on using her until she conceived. And if she didn't, they would strap her down and let the human piece of garbage touch her.

Her throat went tight and she felt faint. She gripped the wall. What did she do? What the hell did she do? She wanted to run. Escape. But how? How would she even try and get out? She had no power here. No cat to sniff her way to freedom. And leaving Hiss...

You will never see Hiss again, fool.

Suddenly, the door fell away. Gia slipped, then caught herself, looked up. The breath left her body.

116

There they all were. The man, the woman and Dax. The latter looked furious, red-faced and breathing hard. Without a word, he grabbed her, yanked her forward and shoved her toward a gurney. She slammed into the mattress and metal, nearly colliding with a surgical tray. Pain lanced through her.

"Easy, Dax," the woman scolded. "She's our new breeder. Our benefactor will not be pleased if you injure one of his pumas."

"She nearly took out my nuts in the elevator," the guard snarled. "I might be permanently injured."

"Hope not," said the man, sliding his gaze to the woman. "If she doesn't get knocked up with the turkey baster, we may just have to send you in. If you get my meaning."

Dax's eyes went from ice to blazing fire in seconds. He understood. All too well.

Never, Gia vowed blackly, her gaze going from the man to the woman to the surgical table, back to Dax.

The grin that touched his mouth as his gaze covetously skimmed her body made her insides wilt.

Never.

Grabbing a blade from the surgical tray, she hacked into both her wrists. No slow death. No chance of recovery. She had to destroy herself before they did it for her.

Sweet pain rushed her like an ocean wave, and just as she was going for her throat, she crumpled to the floor.

CHAPTER 2

Hiss hadn't stopped moving, hadn't stopped pacing his cell since Gia was taken. What the hell were they doing to her? Was it only a blood draw? Or something else?

"Fuck," he growled, slamming his open hand against the bars. Again. He was bruised as hell. But he didn't care.

"Easy," came a male voice behind him. "Some of us are trying to forget about that."

Hiss turned to the male in the cage beside him. "Forget about what?"

"Fucking."

His name was Blade. A former Pantera Suit, who Hiss had never met before coming to the Sub. The male kept mostly to himself. Never had his blood taken. He was required to give other, more intimate samples.

The sound of the elevator descending brought Hiss's head around. He stalked forward, clung to the bars and watched. Finally—it felt like hours—the door opened. Every cell in Hiss's body went numb. Even his cat remained quiet as the two guards walked a very

118

pale, very slow-moving Gia into her cell. Hiss switched to the side of the cage they shared. She looked like hell. Her long blond hair was matted to her beautiful face, the loose strands covering her large, expressive coffee-brown eyes. Her black shirt looked wet in places.

As he tried to will her to look up, look at him, they dumped her on her cot then left without a word. It was only when she let her arms fall to her sides that Hiss saw the true horror of what was done to her. The white, bloodstained bandages around her wrists.

A howl erupted from him, so loud and so fierce, the Sub started to vibrate. Or shit, maybe that was his mind, his skin, his blood. Whatever it was it had unleashed the cat inside him. The cat who had remained docile up until now. He would kill them. Every last one of them for this.

"Hiss," Blade uttered from his cage. "You're going to bring them back down here with dart guns."

Hiss turned and snarled at him. "Let them come."

"Do you want to have her hurt further?" the male returned, his black eyes both understanding and untamed. "You may be ready to fight to the death, but what about Gia?"

The male's words penetrated and hit their mark. *It will come. That time will come.*

"I have to get her out of here," he said.

Blade looked at him as if he were discussing getting to the moon with a paper airplane. But he nodded. "Hell. If you find a way, brother, please take me with you."

Hiss didn't answer. He turned back to Gia. She

looked so small, so thin. How had he let her go with them? Not just this morning, but every goddamned day? It wouldn't happen again. Not while he still breathed.

"Gia?" Hiss called out to her. "Look at me. Please, *ma chère*." *My dear. My darling.*

She didn't move. Her eyes were open, but she was just staring straight ahead. Broken.

With a softer howl, Hiss slid down the bars and dropped on his bare ass. He stuck his arm through, reaching for her. He would wait all day, all night, numb limbs be damned. He didn't give a fuck. And when they came to take his blood again, he would spill theirs instead.

***

She'd failed. And yet she wasn't on the third floor with her feet in the stirrups or Dax on top of her, now was she? Her lip attempted to curl, but she was too tired. And her wrists ached. Not from the cuts, but from the sutures. They hadn't been gentle.

Fuckers.

She blinked a few times, then looked around. Back in her cage. Quiet. No idea what time of day it was. She hadn't eaten a thing, but she wasn't hungry. What now? What would come for her now?

"Why, Gia?"

Hiss's voice. The low, soft timbre was like a tonic for whatever ailed her. Night and day. It was her sustenance. And when she was away from it…well…bad things happened.

"Why what?" she whispered. She was so tired. She just wanted to sleep. An endless sleep.

"Why did they do that to you?" he pressed.

Her head lifted a fraction and her gaze slid to his and she forced an exhausted smile. "They didn't."

As her words and their meaning settled over him, his eyes grew wide with horror, and a low growl rumbled in his chest. The sound was fearsome. Strangely, even more so than the criminals that ran this hellhole.

"Come over here," he commanded blackly. "Crawl if you have to. But come over here right now."

He hadn't yelled. In fact, his voice had never risen above a whisper. But it didn't have to. It was pure animal. The male puma commanding the female. And her instincts compelled her to obey. She got down on the ground and crawled toward him until she was on her knees before the bars. Hiss took both her hands in his. Gently, but forcefully. He didn't even glance at the bandages. His eyes were pinned to hers. They were a formidable stormy gray.

"How dare you," he snarled, keeping his voice low. "You were going to leave me? Leave this motherfucking earth without saying goodbye to me?"

Tears pricked her eyes. "Yes."

His mouth, his beautiful mouth that she'd never even tasted—not even once—formed a hard line.

She forced her chin up. "And if they take me again, I'll try even harder."

"Stop it," he commanded. "Stop talking."

"I'm not going down that way, Hiss. Having some human's semen forced into me. Making me

121

pregnant. Making me have a child. Over and over. And if that doesn't work, letting that piece of shit, Dax, climb on top of me."

Hiss's eyes turned black with rage, and for one brief second Gia thought she saw his cat. It flashed in and out of his features as he bared his teeth.

"Do you understand now?" she whispered.

He nodded. Very slowly. Very deliberately.

"I'm going to get up now," she said. "Go to my cot and stay there. I think it's best if you and I keep away from each other."

"You don't want that," he countered, refusing to let her go.

"Of course I don't. But if they think you mean anything to me, they'll use it to get me on my back. And I don't know if I have the strength to watch you suffer."

She watched her words spear his heart, the heart he always claimed he didn't possess anymore. But she knew what was housed and cared for by his ribs. A male of great feeling and passion and pain.

Her eyes on the bars, she pulled her hand from him. This time he let her. And she stood and slowly made her way back to her cot. She felt his eyes on her as she lay down and curled into herself. Tonight, if she had a nightmare, she would have to do everything in her power to resist the pull of Hiss's warmth...arms...voice...

CHAPTER 3

He hadn't slept. Not for a second. He hadn't allowed it. Guards normally didn't come at night, but he wasn't taking any chances. He'd thought about what he would do if they tried to take her again before his plan could be put in motion. But his ideas weren't very concrete. Without access to the ones taking her, he could do little. So for the rest of the night, he'd prayed it wouldn't come to that. And when the instinctual stirring of dawn broke inside him and the fluorescents flickered on above him, he was thankful.

His eyes went immediately to the cot in the cage next door. She was sleeping on her side, facing him. She looked so soft, so unfettered. Maybe she was dreaming of her home, her Wetlands. Maybe she was dreaming of him. He hadn't heard a peep out of her all night, and at first he'd worried that there was something wrong with her. But moving closer to the bars they shared, he'd heard the deep, even breaths of someone enjoying a solid sleep. She'd needed it.

As if she sensed him watching, or maybe it was the fluorescents, her eyes opened. After a moment, her lips curved into a calm, knowing smile that displayed her incredible strength. She would need it.

They spoke only a little as the morning wore on, honoring her decision that any connection shown between the two of them would lead to an impossible situation for her. But Hiss kept a close eye on her. Even more so when the guards arrived with breakfast. Seated with his back against the brick wall, he painted his entire demeanor in shades of timidity and surrender. But he was ready to spring in case she was taken first.

"A little treat today, kitty cats," Peter called, working his way down the aisle. "Some fruit came in. It's a little rotten, but I know you'll be grateful for it." He gave Hiss a look of disdain as he slipped the bowl under the bars. "You'd better be grateful. Eat up, Ca16," he said, using Hiss's lab name. "Soon as we're done here, Dax and I are taking you upstairs."

He knew Gia was looking at him, but he didn't dare slide his eyes her way. He grabbed the bowl and ate like a madman. Not only did he want to seem compliant, but he also needed the food for strength.

He was nearly done by the time they returned. They hadn't said a word to Gia, hadn't even looked her way. Facts that filled him with an almost desperate relief. It was all on him now. And he wouldn't fail her.

Both Dax and Peter sidled up to his cage, one pulling out his loop of keys while the other unsheathed the dart gun he kept strapped to his thigh. Without being asked, Hiss turned around and put his hands to his sides. Granted, he wasn't known for his cooperation, so he fully expected them to be suspicious.

"Lookie here, Dax," Peter drawled. "It's trying to be docile. What do you make of it?"

Dax snorted. "It saw Br42 come in yesterday. Maybe it got scared. It should be."

Br42. Hiss's gut rolled. Gia was in the breeding program now. Fuck, he had to pull this off. Had to get her out of here. His cat scratched beneath the surface of his skin. *I'm with you,* it seemed to be saying. *Use me. My senses. My strength.*

"Don't you move, Ca16," Peter warned. "Or I swear to god, we'll knock you out. Maybe permanently."

Hiss snarled softly at the bluff. If there was one thing he knew, it was his value. Someone wanted his blood pretty goddamned badly. Same person who'd wanted Reny, no doubt. But to continue with the ruse he put his hands behind his back and dropped his chin to his chest.

"Wise choice," Dax said, though his tone was laced with unease. Always was. The guards in the Sub were chock-full of bravado, but without weapons and bars, they would be torn to bits. And they knew it. "We reward our tame beasts. Maybe an extra plate of food. Or access to a female…"

Hiss not only sensed the dart gun inches away from his neck, but he felt Gia's eyes on him. He wanted to glance her way, reassure her. But he didn't dare. If the idiot behind him pulled the trigger on that gun, the drugs soaked into the dart would take him down in three seconds. And for hours. Maybe days. He didn't have either to waste. So, he waited. He waited until the metal of one cuff brushed his wrist.

Then he struck.

***

At first, Gia thought she was dreaming. That she'd fallen back to sleep after breakfast—or, hell, dreamt that bit too—and was watching Hiss perform what she believed to be an impossible feat. Taking down two human guards with the speed and agility and silence of a shifted cat.

But she still tasted overripe banana on her tongue, and Hiss had grabbed the two dart guns, the keys, and was locking the unconscious and bloody males in his cage and heading over to hers.

She ran to the door, watched him search for the key, then unlock her cage and yank it back.

"Come on," he commanded.

"Hiss! Wait!" It was Blade.

Gia saw the momentary back and forth behind Hiss's eyes. He didn't want to leave her. Even for a moment. But he wasn't going to abandon the other shifters either. Many stood at the doors of their cages, desperately hoping for release. With one quick glance at the guards, Hiss made a break for Blade's cage. But just as he reached it, the elevator started to descend.

"Shit," he growled, working his way through the keys.

"Go," Blade said. "Just go."

Hiss kept at it, faster, faster.

"Goddammit, Hiss," Blade argued. "Go. Take her."

Finally, Hiss shoved the entire set at him. "Hide them. Wait for night, then unlock your cages. I'm coming back with the Pantera. I swear it."

Blade nodded. "We'll be waiting."

Hiss rushed back to Gia, grabbed her hand, and they made a break for the stairs. Hiss tossed her a dart gun as they started to climb. "I don't know what we'll encounter. How many. Just shoot whatever gets in your way."

She nodded, kept sprinting up, one floor, then the next. "Do you know where we're going?"

"Roof."

The word was barely out of his mouth before a door burst open and two human men dressed in lab coats spilled into the stairwell. Hiss shot one in the thigh, and the man went down in an instant. The other looked terrified and tried to run back the way he came. But Gia rushed forward and shot him in the neck.

"He's not going to warn the others," she said, turning to Hiss who was already stripping the larger of the two males.

He dressed quickly, then motioned for Gia to go first. Dart guns ready, they took off up the stairs. Though her wrists stung like bees were attacking them, she could feel the possibility of freedom ahead, and nothing was going to get in her way.

When they finally broke out onto the roof, sunlight assaulted their vision, making them blind for a moment. Gia felt Hiss's hand on hers, squeezing it, leading her forward. She blinked rapidly, trying to acclimate herself to the light. But there wasn't time. Behind them, the door to the roof slammed open.

"Jump, Gia," Hiss commanded. "Now!"

Her vision barely adjusted, Gia did as he asked, trusting him to know that the roof of the adjacent building was truly within their reach.

127

Something whizzed past her head as she leapt. Once, twice. A gasp escaped her throat as she landed with a painful thud, then rolled to the hot tiles. In seconds, Hiss had her back on her feet and they were running to the ledge—then jumping one last time to the rooftop of the building next door.

Once again, she landed with a jarring thud. Her entire body was shaking, humming, and she was pretty sure if she looked down she'd see her wrists were bleeding again. But fuck—they were outside. In fresh air. Free. Free? As Hiss pulled her to her feet, she glanced back, over her shoulder. She'd expected to see figures on the roof of the lab building. But there was no one.

Confused, exhausted, she let Hiss pull her toward the door marked Roof Access, then inside.

"Holy shit," Hiss breathed, pressing back against the metal.

She put her hands on her knees and tried to catch her breath. "What?"

"We're in Baton Rouge. This is the Chancey Hotel."

He sounded both relieved and pained. "So we're close to your home?"

He didn't answer. His eyes were pinned to her arms, her wrists. She looked down, not surprised to see that her bandages were stained with blood.

"I'm fine," she assured him, standing up, ready to go.

"You need a doctor," he said, taking her hand gently and guiding to the stairwell. "And I need to speak with Raphael."

"Who's he?"

"The leader of the Pantera. And one of many who would love to see me return to the Wildlands. Only so he can see the light go out of my eyes when he kills me."

CHAPTER 4

The land beneath Hiss's feet hummed with energy and magic, and the air was scented of autumn on the bayou—a season that had to beg and plead with summer for emancipation. But Goddess, when it did come on, and those browns and oranges, reds and yellows emerged, nothing in the whole world could rival its beauty.

Hiss ventured a glance in Gia's direction as they walked. It was good to see her in nature, his nature, the late afternoon sun shining on her long yellow hair, her skin still very pale, but with a hint of color on her cheeks. It had taken them a good two hours to get picked up by a trucker after slinking out of Baton Rouge via several back alleys, but the ride had given him time to tend to her wounds. He'd managed to stop the bleeding, and the decent male trucker had given her a spare jacket and a pair of his wife's sneakers to keep.

"Are you happy to be going home?" she asked him as they followed the curve of the bayou.

"I'm happy to be with you," he said. "To be free." *For as long as that lasts.*

"Well that's sweet and evasive." She gave a curious smile.

Answers and explanations. His recent history with the males and females on the other side of the bayou. He exhaled thickly. All those nights when Gia had needed him, when she'd bared her soul, talked of her former life, and he'd given back so little. Not because he didn't want to share himself with her, but because he was afraid if he did, she'd despise him. She was Pantera, though her sect called themselves Cadejo. And to their race, loyalty was everything. How would she react when she realized he lacked the one trait she valued above all others?

His gaze kicked up, took in all the colors of home, the scents, where he'd run and played and guarded. They were about to cross over into that world. It was a world that despised him now. His lip curled. He didn't want her to hear about his crimes from anyone else but him.

"I am happy to be home," he began tentatively. "But my Pantera family won't be as happy to see me."

"I gathered," she said. "You've dropped a few clues over the past few days. Can you tell me why?"

He wrapped an arm around her waist and took her with him as he maneuvered over a fallen log. "I made a mistake, Gia. A grave mistake. I allowed my anger and bitterness against three to bring danger and shame to the rest. I was blind to everything else. Pantera were hurt because of me. I betrayed my clan. Worked with the enemy against my clan."

She stopped, her eyes searching his as the light filtered through a stand of moss-covered cypress. "There must've been a reason."

"Maybe so, but that's no excuse, is it?"

"Not an excuse, but an explanation." Her hand came up and she brushed his jaw. "I know you," she said with passion. "I know your heart. Your goodness."

I was good for you. Only you.

"Understand," he said, avoiding the backstory she wanted so much to hear. "They will take me into custody the moment I step foot on Wildlands soil."

Her fingers froze on his cheek and her eyes narrowed. "Then why are we going here?"

He turned into her hand and kissed her palm. He'd never known anyone like her. "I promised Blade, and the rest. I can't leave them there. I won't."

Her eyes softened. "See? Goodness. Heart."

All he saw was her, and how amazing she was. He didn't deserve her. But he hoped, one day, he would. He took her hand in his and urged her onward through the marsh, crossing over the bayou on the secret footpath he and his Hunter peers had used a thousand times. They were so close. He felt it. His cat certainly felt it.

As they drew deeper into the cover of the trees, the need to shift was a living thing, powerful, like a sweet drug. But Hiss knew if wanted any chance of explaining his presence to whoever was patrolling the borders, he needed to remain in his male form.

He would save his cat in case one of the Pantera attempted to touch, intimidate or harm the female beside him.

Gia stopped then and inhaled sharply.

"What is it?" Hiss demanded, scanning her. "Your wrists? Are you in pain?"

She shook her head. "I feel it. It's…incredible." A smile breaking on her beautiful face, she lifted her eyes to meet his.

Hiss's insides flared with heat. Predatory heat. Yes, they were inside the Wildlands now. Normally a deep, dark brown, Gia's eyes now glowed with the color of an amber stone. His cat rumbled in his chest. It wanted out. It wanted to nuzzle and sniff and lick. First Gia.

Then her cat.

"Come," he growled, forcing back the desire flickering inside him, and leading her deeper into the bayou, until they reached the ancient ginkgo.

There Hiss paused, looked up at the tree, its many leaves turned a bright, welcoming yellow. As the scent snaked into his nostrils, he tightened his grip on Gia's hand.

"You have some serious balls coming back here, Hiss."

Hiss didn't even need to turn around to know who was addressing him. After all, they'd worked side by side for decades. But he gave the leader of the Hunters his respect, and faced him.

Fierce gold eyes slammed into his.

Hiss acknowledged the look with a grim smile. "Hello, Parish."

***

"Where is he?" Gia demanded fiercely as she paced back and forth in front of the leader of the Pantera.

They were in his office, and the stunning blond male with sharp, assessing eyes the color of gold-flecked jade remained seated, watching her. After the one called Parish had brought them to the Suits' Headquarters, a virtual army of Pantera had descended on Hiss. With his grim consent and a nod of acceptance flashed her way, they'd taken him, and Raphael had "escorted" her here.

She didn't know these Pantera. Didn't know how they worked. Whether they were in any way a merciful sect. But the second Hiss was out of her sight, she couldn't quell the anxiety in her blood. If they hurt him…

"He's meeting with our Hunters," Raphael told her. And as if reading her mind, added, "No harm will come to him." He raised his brow and said very pointedly, "Yet."

Her lips curled up.

Raphael interlocked his fingers and let his chin rest on his knuckles. "I want to know about you, Gia. About where you come from…where you were before the lab. Have you been living among humans?"

For a moment, she thought about holding back. Why did this male deserve her truth? Maybe she would bargain with him for it. Truth for Hiss. But the leader of the Pantera didn't seem the bargaining kind. And she didn't want her tenacity to cost Hiss in the end.

"My family come from a sect in the Everglades. As you are Pantera, we are Cadejo."

Raphael nodded, but didn't seem surprised by the information. Or the name. Her brows knit together.

134

"And did you know of the Pantera before you met Hiss?" he asked.

"No."

"How were you taken? Was it from your home?"

Gia wanted to tell him she didn't remember, but she wasn't sure she could lie that well. The day would live in her memory, in her nightmares, for eternity. "I was in Miami selling alligator hide. I go once a month." She shrugged. "We eat a lot of alligator in the Wetlands. I was loading the hide into the buyer's van when I was struck with a needle. I woke up in the Sub."

"And you were a blood donor?"

"So to speak," she answered tightly.

His eyes flickered to her hands, her wrists. "How are you healing, by the way?"

Without even a hint of embarrassment or shame, Gia held out her arms. "Very well. The magic is incredibly strong and pure here. As it is at home."

A flash of interest lit his eyes, but again, he didn't probe the subject of the Cadejo. She wondered at it. Learning of a new group of puma shifters had to birth all sorts of questions. Unless it wasn't his first time hearing of it.

"Have you been able to shift here?" he asked

"I haven't had a chance to try," she told him with a lift to her chin. "With the swift capture and now the interrogation. Who knows what lies ahead."

His lips twitched. "You are suspicious of me."

"Of course I am. I don't know you."

"But you know Hiss," he countered.

"Yes."

He sniffed with derision.

"Is that so impossible to believe?" she pushed.

"You don't have a clue who that male really is, Gia. If you did—"

"A traitor, right?" she interrupted. She crossed her arms over her chest and regarded him. "Is that what he is? All that he is?"

Raphael blanched. "He told you."

"Of course he told me."

"And that doesn't…concern you?" he asked, his voice a low growl on the last two words.

"What concerns me is his well-being." She arched a brow at him. "I want to see him."

"He's busy."

"Being tortured? I promised, I won't interrupt."

"I'm sorry, Gia, but you don't understand—"

"No, you don't understand," she countered blackly. "He is my mate."

That pronouncement brought with it a full minute of silence, and Raphael's stunned expression. Or was it a horrified glare? Frankly, Gia didn't care. She'd said what was true in her heart. What she wanted. Maybe it hadn't been spoken between them. But she and Hiss had bonds and ties that went far beyond spoken words or declarations.

"In my sect," she continued, "mate status comes with certain rights and privileges."

"In ours as well," Raphael acknowledged. "But your male," he said on a sneer, "is our prisoner. And prisoners don't have rights. They have cages."

A shudder went through her and she had to fight to keep herself steady and in control. "Hiss and I know a good deal about living in cages."

136

The male's jaw tightened. "You, of course, will be treated as a welcome and honored guest. There are plenty of places to stay in the Wildlands. You have only to choose—"

"I choose him," she interrupted. "If Hiss stays in a cage, then I will stay with him."

Those gold eyes flashed with curiosity. "You are very stubborn."

"You have no idea."

"Hiss told you he was a traitor. Did he tell you what he did? How the lives of his family, and by that I mean the Pantera, were put in danger? We lost a life, Gia."

"I'm very sorry for that." She wouldn't make excuses for him. She didn't need to. Hiss was well aware of what he'd done. He lived with it every second of every day. "But he also saved a life," she added.

"Whose?" Raphael sneered.

"Mine."

His mouth opened, but he said nothing.

"And he could save many more, we both could, if you'd act on the information we've brought you." She sighed. "Think about it for one second, Leader of the Pantera. He came back here. Knowing the risks, knowing his certain fate, so he could save not only my life but everyone in that building in Baton Rogue. You want to know my first thought when we escaped? Getting home. Getting to my family. Now." She went to the door and opened it. "I want to see my mate."

For a solid minute, Raphael digested what she'd said to him. Tension flickered in the air around them.

But finally, he nodded. "Very well, Gia of the Cadejo.
Follow me." He stood up, shifted into his cat and
growled at her to follow him.

CHAPTER 5

In a conference room on the top floor of the Suits' Headquarters, the Hunters—Hiss's once-upon-a-time Hunters—surrounded him a tight semi-circle. Not to reminisce or to chastise him. But to get their questions answered. How long had he been at the lab? Were there any other Wildlands Pantera there? What seemed to be their goal? How many floors were there? How many guards? Had he ever heard the name Christopher? Why did they want his blood?

As he answered, his gaze moved over each one in turn. Parish, Keira, Mal, Bayon and Lena. They had been his friends once upon a time. Ran side by side with his puma. They'd trusted him with their lives. And he could see it in their eyes. That trust was gone.

"Mal, draw us up a map," Parish commanded. "We'll meet to strategize at midnight. Let's hope the building's not already burned to the ground like the rest of Stanton's properties by the time we get there."

"It won't be," Hiss assured him.

"How can you be so sure?" Bayon put in. "It's how he rolls."

"Yes," Mal agreed. "But remember what the human, Chelsea, has told us. Stanton Locke had one last big lab left in the South. He wouldn't tell her or anyone else where it was because they couldn't spare it. I don't think they'd risk burning it down over a couple of test subjects going missing."

"Agreed," Hiss said, easily falling into his old way of talking to his peers. That is, until both Lena and Parish tossed him a vile sneer.

Mal, who had once been a great friend of his, asked, "And you say they know we're coming, Hiss? The prisoners?"

He nodded, his chest tight when she refused to look him directly in his eyes. "I gave one of them, Blade is his name, the keys. Told him to make sure all cages were unlocked tonight."

"Blade?" came a new voice to the fold.

Hiss glanced up. Raphael was standing inside the doorway, and just behind him was Gia. A wave of relief spilled through him when she gave him a reassuring smile.

"You know him, Raph?" Parish asked.

"He's a Pantera Suit. Worked undercover out of New York, Boston and Florida." The male looked pained. "We need to get them out of there."

The leader of the Hunters turned back to Hiss. "How many cats on the lowest level?"

"Twelve."

"Plus how many on the higher floors?"

Hiss shook his head. "I could only guesstimate. Twenty, thirty? Children and human prisoners too."

Keira inhaled sharply. "Those soulless fuckers."

"We'll make sure they pay, sis," Parish assured his twin.

"What will we do with them?" Lena asked. "When we bring them back here? Where will we put them?"

"Indy has plans for housing along the eastern border," Raphael answered. "But in the meantime, we'll use Medical, here, boarding, spare rooms, whatever's available."

The Hunters nodded in unison.

"I think that's all for now," Parish said. "The rest of you can go." His gaze slid to Hiss. "I'll make sure the prisoner gets to his cell. The elders have already been notified of his capture."

It was the first time Hiss had allowed a growl to escape his lips since he'd been back. But it brought the attention of all the Hunters. Bayon started toward him, but only managed a few steps before Gia pushed past Raphael and came to stand at Hiss's side.

Her chin lifted, she grabbed his hand. "We're ready."

***

"Not exactly the cages we're used to, is it?" Gia remarked as they stood in the living room of the small but well-appointed cottage at the foot of the bayou.

"This isn't for me," Hiss said tightly.

"What do you mean?" She turned around to look at him. He'd changed into a pair of navy sweats and a matching t-shirt. It seemed strange to see him in clothes. But they fit very well, stretching over and across his lean, muscular body.

His eyes caught and held hers. "Raphael wants to make sure that when you return home you report only positive treatment by the Pantera. He is a Diplomat, after all."

When *we* return home? she wanted to suggest. But she kept the thought to herself. Hiss would love the Wetlands. And he would be free of censure there. They could start over... Hell, they could just start.

"But make no mistake," he continued. "It may feel calm and comfortable and hidden here, but there are guards all around us."

She sobered somewhat, walked over to him. "What is their plan for you, do you think? A trial? Captivity? Will you be drugged so that your cat cannot emerge?" She shivered at that last question. She couldn't imagine never being able to shift. It had been hell over the past several months. Not being able to connect with her cat.

"I honestly don't know," he said. "Whatever it is, I deserve it. I accept it."

She wrapped her arms around his waist, looked up at him. "Tell me. Tell me why you did what you did."

He stared down at her. "Does it matter?"

"Not with regard to how I feel about you. But I want to know. I want to know you. Your heart, your pain. You barely shared that side of yourself with me."

"It's an ugly side."

She sniffed. "Baby, we all have those. And anyone who says differently is a liar." She snuggled into his chest. Being in his arms, this close to him without bars in their way, was pure heaven. "I just

142

don't want us to have any secrets. It won't work if we do."

"What won't work?" he asked, his lips against her hair.

"Our mating."

He stilled.

She smiled. "I want to mate you, Hiss."

A growl rumbled through him. She felt it against her chest, against the tips of her breasts, and it made her belly clench deliciously.

"And as you know," she continued, lifting her head, "if I want something badly enough I get it."

His eyes were a rich smoky gray. They clung to hers and his nostrils flared. He was drawing her scent.

"Kiss me," she urged. "You want to, don't you?"

His gaze dropped to her mouth and a soft snarl escaped his lips. "Oh, Gia, I've wanted to since that first night. But…"

"No buts," she said, heat flickering between their tightly pressed bodies. "Look where we are. How we are. I'm holding you, you're holding me. No bars between us, no nightmares, no—"

Hiss's mouth was on hers before she could get that last word out. And as he kissed her with feral hunger and unbridled passion, life outside the cottage, outside the circle that their bodies made, didn't exist. It was only heat and moans, skin and friction. Gia was overcome, overwhelmed. She wanted to both consume him and be consumed by him. And yet, she couldn't decide which she wanted first. Her mind was butterflies on the bayou, flitting and floating, while her back arched and her hips pressed against the rigid arousal in his sweats.

Never in her life had she been kissed this way. All in, all consuming, starving. Like neither of them had eaten in weeks. Not the kind of food that would sustain them, anyway. Bland, boring, barely edible. This was the highly spiced, gourmet fare, addictive as hell.

She moaned and dipped her tongue into his mouth to play and lap, laughing when he slammed her tighter against him in response. Crushing her sensitive breasts against his hard chest. Every inch of her was hot and humming, and between her thighs she felt slick.

He pulled back and bit her lower lip. "Your scent is making me insane, Gia."

"More," was her response, growling against his mouth. "You. Naked. Me. Too."

He cursed, picking her up easily and stalking toward the couch. Anticipation filled her. She reached down and grabbed the edges of his shirt. *Off.* She needed it off. That's how he was supposed to be. Gloriously naked.

And aroused.

Goddess, she couldn't wait to see it. His cock, standing proud. Wanting her. Waiting to fill her.

She felt herself falling, and for a second her panic response kicked in. But Hiss had her, eased her down until her back was touching soft, pliant cushion.

"You sure about this?" he asked, poised above her, his expression a mask of ferocious hunger.

Her sex tingled, hummed, craved. "You're kidding, right?"

A cocky grin touched his mouth. She wanted to bite that mouth. And she would. Later.

"How the fuck did I get so lucky?" he uttered, pulling off his shirt. "Best day of my life when I was put in the Sub next to you."

"Don't," she begged. "Don't go there."

"You changed me, Gia. Humbled me. I thought I was the only one suffering…" He yanked off his shirt, tossed it away.

Yes. Yes. That. Me. You.

So insanely aroused, so insanely desperate for him to stop talking and claim her mouth again as he claimed her body, she hardly heard the knock on the door.

But Hiss heard it.

He was up and off her, and changing into his cat in seconds. It was the first time Gia had seen him shift, and for a moment, she just stared at the auburn puma. It was massive, intimidating, its shoulders nearly as wide as the door he was heading for.

"Wait," she called.

He stopped and glanced back. Silver eyes bore a hole in her head before he snarled. *Stay back,* he seemed to be saying. And Gia's insides liquefied once again. She was female. He was male.

The knock came again, and Hiss's cat growled and returned to its task, stalking to the door. Once there, his mouth closed around the knob, and he turned his head. With a snarl, he pulled back the door.

A stunning dark-haired female stood there, dressed in a black tank top and tight-fitting blue jeans. The second she saw Hiss's cat, her face lit up.

"Hiss."

Gia watched as he quickly shifted back into his

145

male form. He stared at the female. "Oh, Goddess. Reny."

She didn't say a word. Just launched herself at him. Arms going around his neck, a sound of pure pleasure exiting her mouth.

That's when Gia stood up. And for the first time in six months, her cat came out to play.

CHAPTER 6

It had taken him time, patience and quite a bit of brawn to calm down his sexy little puma, get her to shift back and listen to him. But when he did, and when she realized that the female standing in their doorway was his sister, Gia had reacted as only Gia could: with a hug for Reny, an apology, and a push for them to go out on the porch and have some alone time together while she took a well-deserved shower.

The visual had been difficult for Hiss to walk away from. But in truth, this was the first time he and Reny had met on an even playing field, so to speak. The last time he'd seen her, spoken to her, he'd been imprisoned on the island of lost Pantera. And by lost, he meant the small cabin where uncontrolled cats and traitors to their kind were sent. He hadn't been very kind or welcoming to Reny then. Anger and bitterness and resentment did that to a body. So did shock—as he wasn't expecting to hear that his sister, who he'd mourned for too many years to count—was alive. But he was a different male now, and he was so grateful to see her. Who knew when that would happen again?

If it would happen again.

His gaze traveled over her face, seeking to find resemblances and memories. Those intelligent green eyes had belonged to their father. And the wicked smile that lit up her entire face mirrored his own…well, once upon a time anyway. When he'd felt the carefree puma, the purposeful Hunter, the steadfast friend.

"You know I was warned off seeing you," she said. They were seated on the steps of the porch, the sun gently setting in shades of peach and copper. "Sebastian was afraid you'd hurt me."

Hiss released a soft growl. He hated to think she would ever believe him capable of such a thing.

"He didn't mean physically," she clarified. "Break my heart kind of thing." She smiled that smile. The wicked, teasing one. "I don't think he understands how important you are to me. How this connection is vital to my happiness. It's family." She glanced out at the water. "When you were gone, taken, and I thought I'd never see you again, I felt such grief."

Hiss's chest tightened, and he reached out and covered her hand with his. He hated that she felt pain, but he was also pleased that she valued him at all.

"When I heard you'd come back," she said, looking at him again, "the happiness I felt, the relief…it was palpable. But I have to say, I'm still pretty shocked that you did. After everything…"

"Yeah," he said with a wry grin. "You're not the only one who feels that way. Now the Pantera think I'm a fool as well as a traitor."

"They don't know what to think," she said. "After all that's happened, your anger at the elders, working with Shakpi's followers, being taken captive, saving that female's life—and returning here, to certain imprisonment, to save the lives of those captives… It's hard to make a judgment with so many factors at play."

He could tell she was looking for answers, an explanation for the mercurial range of behaviors. He released her hand, but not her gaze. "Losing you, losing the family in that way, so young…" he started. "It nearly destroyed me. I was alone. To think and grow bitter, and blame. Do you know what the elders told me?"

She shook her head.

"That you and Mom and Dad had been exposed as shifters to the human world, and were in danger. But instead of sending help, bringing you home to me, they left you to fend for yourselves. Not wanting to expose the Pantera any further. They told me you'd been killed. A fire."

Her eyes shuttered. "Maybe that's what they believed?" she offered. "Maybe that's what they'd been told. I don't excuse their callous way of dealing with the fears of having the Pantera exposed. That is truly heartless, and they should admit to it. But maybe that's not why Mom and Dad died. Maybe the fire was just—"

"No." His one-word interruption caused her to startle.

"You don't think their death was an accident?"

Hiss stared at her, debating. He could hardly tell her that he believed he'd seen their mother, been cared for in the lab by her. Without proof, he'd sound insane.

"Truly, I don't know what happened to them," he said finally. "But I know the elders sent no one to help. Them or you." He shook his head, cursed. "You might not have been exposed to years of abuse and torture if they… Goddess help me, Reny, I had weeks of that and my head's not on straight. I doubt it ever will be. I don't know how you…"

"I'm okay, Hiss," she assured him with such vehemence that he couldn't not believe it was true. "When it came back, all the memories, it was difficult for sure. I still dream about it, still wake up wondering where I am. But I manage. And Sebastian, my mate, he makes me feel so safe. So loved." Her eyes warmed. "Is that how you feel with Gia?"

Just the sound of her name made his breath stall in his lungs and his pulse jump. He glanced over his shoulder at the screen door. "When I no longer cared if I breathed another day in that hole in the lab, Gia made me want to live again. She made me believe I could be better, different. Useful. Forgiven. With all I've done, what I've destroyed, I don't deserve her, and yet I strive to."

His sister's eyes moved over his face. "I hate that the elders turned their back on our family. Failed our family. But as you and I know all too well, bad things happen. Choices are made for reasons that seem just, yet are petty and selfish, even cruel. On all sides," she said pointedly. She exhaled heavily. "I don't know, brother. Maybe I'm just saying…stop. Let it go. Ask for forgiveness, accept it if it's granted and live the best life you can now. Because I want to know you. I want my children, if I'm ever that lucky, to know you."

His gut was aching something fierce. So much pain,

that he'd endured—and that he'd caused. "I want that too," he uttered. "It's why I'm here. Why I came back."

A smile touched her lips. It was like looking in the mirror for a moment. "I've found you again, brother, and I'm so grateful."

"As am I, sister," he said, moving closer to her, dropping an arm across her shoulders.

She let her head fall to his, and for a good half hour they sat there in companionable silence, watching the sun descend into the bayou.

***

Gia hadn't seen a real bed with clean sheets and a warm comforter in months. So after her shower, she'd decided to stretch out and relax for a few minutes while Hiss and his sister reconnected outside. Not surprisingly though, that stretch had extended to sliding underneath the covers. And the relax bit? Well, that had morphed into a good old-fashioned catnap.

One that was being deliciously interrupted by a hot, hard male body sidling up behind her.

She instantly pressed back against him and sighed. His chest was bare, but he was still wearing his sweats. She wanted those off. Wanted him naked and rubbing against her.

"Sleeping without me, Gia?" he whispered, brushing her still-damp hair off her neck with his cool fingers, then leaning in to plant a kiss on her pulse point. "Naughty kitten."

Eyes still closed, she grinned. "I know. How will you punish me?"

A growl vibrated near her ear. "I can think of a few ideas."

She shivered.

"But first, the guards brought dinner," he said, licking the shell of her ear, then biting down hard on the lobe. She gasped and arched her back, felt his impressively hard cock at the base of her spine.

"I have it on the table," he continued. "You hungry?"

Heat was swirling through her now and her mind was slow and soft. "Not for food," she managed.

"Yeah," he uttered. "Me neither."

The heat and hardness of him left her momentarily, and she felt the covers being pulled away. Frustrated, heady with lust, she rolled to her back to see what was going on. Demand that he return to her. But he already had. He was positioned over her like a predatory animal, his steely gray gaze pinning her where she was.

"In my bed," he growled. "Where you belong, Gia. You know that, don't you? Understand that?"

Breathless, she nodded.

"Tell me," he commanded. "I need to hear you say it."

"This is where I belong, Hiss. In your bed. With you. Under you."

His brow arched. "On my tongue?"

Her sex tightened and she canted her hips.

"What about on my fingers?" he demanded. "Your sweet cream coating my fingers?"

"Oh, Goddess," she breathed. "Yes, yes, yes. Please, Hiss. I can't take it anymore."

"You never have to beg me, Gia." He smiled. "Not more than once, anyway." With deft fingers, he untied the knot of her white robe and spread the cotton flaps wide, revealing her nude body to his gaze. At first, he just stared, skimming her from face to neck, to shoulders to breasts to waist... But when those two gray orbs settled on her sex, which she'd shaved bare in the shower tonight, his nostrils flared and for a second she saw his cat shift in and out of his features.

It made her wild with lust. Every muscle in her body going tense, ready, waiting for his command. She was a puma female and she loved when Hiss showed her his Pantera male fierceness.

"Did you do this to tempt me, Gia?" he asked, his eyes sliding up to meet hers.

"You bet your ass I did, Hiss," she shot back, then smiled wickedly.

"It wasn't necessary," he said, dropping his head and kissing her mouth. "The sweet scent of your pussy has been driving me insane for weeks." He started moving down her body. One hand fisted her breast, while his mouth hovered above the other. "I need no more encouragement."

Gia was hardly breathing. She was stiff. Dying to be touched, licked, eaten.

"However..." As his right hand kneaded her breasts, he nuzzled the other with his nose, then flicked the tight bud with his tongue. "It is a most tempting sight."

She inhaled sharply and canted her hips again. "Hiss, please. You're being cruel."

He laughed, his hot breath teasing her wet,

sensitive nipple. "I'm savoring, *ma chère*. Every delectable inch. And you are that...delectable." He sucked her nipple into his mouth hard.

Gia grabbed his head, threaded his hair with her fingers and growled.

"Your pussy had better be soaking wet by the time I get to it, Gia," he warned, his tone savage, guttural. "Or else I may not put my mouth on you." He lowered his head and kissed her ribs, then her belly. "Do you have enough cream for me, kitten?"

Back arched, fingers digging into Hiss's scalp, Gia was one strung-out nerve ending. She was afraid that one lick of Hiss's sharp, demanding tongue and she would come. Goddess, she didn't want that. She'd dreamed about this moment. Being taken by this male. It wouldn't be momentary bliss.

His fingers scraped gently down her lower abdomen and over her shaved pussy. She moaned and bucked, so sensitive it was almost torturous. Almost. And then he dropped his head and kissed her. One soft kiss on the seam of her sex.

"Hiss," she breathed.

"Yes, *ma chère*," he uttered, his tongue making one long swipe from the opening of her pussy to her clit. "Not to worry. You are most definitely wet enough. It pleases me. You are a good kitten."

His tongue was on her again, gently circling her aching bud. It was too much. Her body...her breath...she was going to come.

"No," she cried out, abandoning his hair and gripping his shoulders. "No. Please. Hiss. No."

He stiffened and pulled his head back. "What's

wrong, Gia? You don't want me to touch you? Lick you? Tell me."

Gia cursed herself. She hadn't meant it that way. "Of course I want you to touch me," she cried out. "But I need to touch you too. Taste you while you taste me."

He groaned.

"Give me your cock, Hiss."

For a few seconds, he didn't move. Then he cursed and repositioned himself so she had access to him. Hungry, happy, and insanely excited, she rolled to her side, grabbed the waistband of his sweats and yanked them down.

Oh, Goddess, yes. This was what she wanted. All of him. Every glorious hard inch of—

Her thoughts died there because Hiss had her pussy spread wide and his mouth was on her again, his lips suckling gently on her clit. Heat surged to every cell of her body. Heat and mind-stealing pleasure. She fisted his cock and dropped her head. As she sucked him, reveling in the thickness of him and the taste of him, he consumed her. Lapping at her cream, circling her bud, then flattening his tongue and thrusting up. Over and over. Again and again until she was panting and bucking against his mouth.

"Oh fuck, Gia," he groaned.

She drew on him tighter and faster, loving how worked-up she was making him, loving the taste of his salty pre-come on her tongue.

And then he slid two fingers inside her and she was done for.

Fucking her slowly as he licked her, Hiss thrust

into her mouth. They were both a wild mass of hunger and need.

Crying out, Gia broke apart. She was like an animal possessed, riding his mouth as she sucked him off.

"I'm going to come," Hiss warned her, trying to pull away.

But she held him fast. She wanted his come, wanted to taste him, drink him down. And with three furious, deep thrusts to the back of her throat, she got her wish.

Hot seed cascading down her throat.

Minutes later, Hiss had his head to the pillow and was pulling her into his arms. "Just breathe, *ma chère*," he uttered. "I have you. Always will have you."

She snuggled up against him, feeling satiated and tired, and hungry for him. For him inside of her. Her mind felt altered somehow. Shaken and stirred, and yet her heart felt indescribably full and happy.

"I feel as though I waited a lifetime for that," Hiss uttered, kissing the top of her head. "For you."

She smiled, loving how vulnerable he was being with her. She hoped it would extend to everything else in their lives. Fears, plans, the past...

"How did it go with your sister?" she began gingerly, her arm draped across his chest.

He sighed. "It was good. To see her, talk with her. There was so much I needed to say, explain. She didn't know all that had happened when she was gone. What the elders told me about her and Mom and Dad."

"Was she upset?"

"She was surprised. But she has moved forward, and she urged me to do the same."

"Do you think that's possible?" she asked, then held her breath.

"I do." His arms tightened around her. "Now I do."

It was all they said. Their bodies were weary. Not from the pleasure they'd just experienced, but from hours and days and weeks of pain and torture and living breath-to-breath.

As she closed her eyes and let her body relax completely and utterly for the first time in a long time, Gia felt loved and safe and cherished.

For the first time in a long time, she fell asleep with a smile on her lips.

CHAPTER 7

Hiss hadn't slept.

He'd wanted to. With Gia wrapped in his arms, her near-nude body draped across his. Fuck yeah, he wanted to fall asleep. Then wake up the next the morning, maybe before dawn, and sink into the hot, wet sheath he'd been so fortunate to taste tonight. But he had a promise to keep.

One he was sure the Leader of the Pantera was going to fight him on.

Just before midnight, Hiss had sent one of his guards to fetch Raphael. He'd offered to go himself, but the two fairly green yet overly rule-rigid Hunters hadn't enjoyed that idea. So Hiss had waited, stood at the edge of the bayou, under the moon's clear light. If he went back into the cottage he was afraid he'd crawl right back into bed with Gia.

"Summoning me?" came a taut male voice behind him. "And just as I was saying goodbye to my mate."

Hiss turned. "You're going on the mission?"

"No. But I'll be at Headquarters monitoring the entire thing." The male's eyebrow drifted up. "I haven't heard an apology. I don't look kindly on interruptions with my mate before a battle. Unless of course it's the glorious squawk of one called Soyala."

Hiss inclined his head. "I'm sorry. I left mine as well. So I understand your frustration."

"Then tell me, why are we here?"

Hiss glanced at the guards bracketing him. "Can we speak in private?"

"You can go," Raphael told the males, then stepped forward, closing the distance between himself and Hiss. "I grow weary."

"I have to go on this mission," Hiss told him.

"Prisoners don't go on missions," he countered. "You know that." His eyes narrowed. "Is that why you brought me out here?"

"This is different. You need me there. You need all the Hunters you can get."

The male's eyes flashed with unrest. "That's why I have a full team of Hunters coming. None of this should concern you. You're not a Hunter."

The words hurt. Cut deep. Because to Hiss, he would always be a Hunter. The title, his genetic makeup, it didn't just go away because he'd fucked up. Or did it?

He exhaled heavily. "So what's the plan then, Raphael? Keep me captive here? Or in a cage lined with malachite? Or maybe you'll feed me to the bayou and be done with it once and for all?"

The Suit's brows lifted a fraction. "That sounds interesting."

Hiss turned away and cursed. "I know what I've done. What I've caused. How I lost my way. Let me earn back the title of Hunter." His eyes came back to the male and they were brimming with the passion of his cat. "Just this one night. I know my way around the lab. But more importantly, I made a promise to Blade and the others. I also swore vengeance on those assholes." His nostrils flared and his gut tightened. "They had Gia, Raph. Were about to force a pregnancy on her." His lip curled. "Any way they could."

Raphael growled. "Fuck me."

"And she wasn't alone in that. They're making hybrids in there. For blood, for power. I don't know. But the suffering is horrifying." A cold wind whipped up around them and a cloud shaded the moon. "The puma in the Sub know me, trust me—yes, I realize what I'm saying, and how impossible it sounds to you."

Raphael stared at him. Hard. "I don't know…"

"I can't allow her to love me this way."

"And what way is that?" Raphael asked, his jaw working.

"As a traitor." He inhaled sharply. "Let me try and change that moniker. Or do penance for it, at least."

"How do I know you won't run?"

"Because Gia is here."

The simple, truthful, vulnerable answer stalled the leader's anger and bluster. He glanced past Hiss to the cottage. Then exhaled, shook his head slightly. "I must be insane to even be contemplating this."

"Or just…curious?"

Raphael's gold eyes narrowed on him. "If you try to run," he warned, "the Hunters will shoot to kill."

Hiss nodded. "Understood."

160

"Come with me." He started walking away from the bayou. Then stopped. "Will you say goodbye to your female?"

Hiss glanced up at the cottage. "I don't want to wake her." Every inch of him, the blood in his veins, all wanted to be back with her. In his bed. He turned back to Raphael. "Can you do me one last favor?"

***

It wasn't a nightmare that woke her this time, but a hunger for Hiss. Her mate. The male who had sent her flying and reeling and…just over the moon.

She wanted more.

Craved more.

Saying his name, she reached for him, searched the other side of the bed for him, and the feel of that hot skin over steely muscle. Right now she wanted the muscle between his legs. She was so ready. But her search came up empty.

She sat up and turned on the light. Her gaze moved about the room. What time was it? There was no clock in the bedroom.

Slipping out of bed, she re-tied her robe and headed for the living room. The house was so quiet, bathroom was vacant, and inside her chest, her heart started to thump.

"Hiss?" she called, rubbing the sleep from her eyes. It was dark except for a single light coming from the kitchen area. She followed it.

But again, he wasn't there.

A thread of panic moved through her now. She

stared up at the clock. It was two in the morning. Where the hell was he? Had someone taken him? She was just about to head to the front door, see if maybe he was out on the porch or down by the bayou or checking up on the guards, when she spotted a piece of paper on the counter near the sink.

Instantly she snatched it up. As she read, her heart started to ache with anger and frustration and longing. He was gone. Of his own accord. To the lab in Baton Rogue with the other Hunters.

She stared at the paper. At his messy scrawl. *You damn bastard. Leaving a female in your bed without saying goodbye.*

She read the note over again, one last time, then tossed it in the trash and returned to bed.

She'd learned a grave lesson. It was time to call her family.

CHAPTER 8

The building was dark, seemingly shut down for the night—maybe even for good. As the wind swirled around him, Hiss stared at the place that had held him captive, drained his life's blood. The place that had given him Gia. Dark. Like nothing truly lived within it. But Hiss knew what was happening behind those walls—those thick walls stained with blood and tears. So much pain, so much fear. And his puma brothers and sisters, waiting.

"We should've used a helicopter," Keira remarked as they all spilled out onto the roof of the Chancey Hotel.

"Right," Hakan answered dryly. "Because that wouldn't alert them to our presence or anything." He shot Hiss a grin.

Though momentarily surprised, Hiss returned the gesture. For too many years to count, Hakan had been his closest friend, and the one Hiss had felt devastated about disappointing. It was good to know the male was giving him a chance at redemption. The other Hunters on the mission were acting as if he didn't belong. Even though he had fallen back into their ways, their rhythm, seamlessly.

163

"Keira," Parish said, standing on the edge of the parapet. "You need to get that fear of heights under control." And to really send the point home, he jumped to the roof of the building next door with ridiculous ease.

A few of the Hunters laughed, especially after Parish turned around, grinned and beckoned them all onward.

Keira cursed at him under her breath, but managed to stick not only the first jump, but the second, landing softly on the roof of the lab with the rest of the Hunters.

"Quiet now," Parish commanded as they headed for the door.

As expected, it was locked, but Rosalie made quick work of it. She was exceptional at breaking and entering, and Hiss wished he could tell her so. But the Hunter hadn't spoken to him or even glanced his way since Raphael had brought him in for the mission. Not that he blamed her. His choices had led to the death of her mate, Mercier. Odds were that she wouldn't ever see it in her heart to forgive him. But even so, he would always have her back.

With the door unlocked and propped open, Parish stood just inside it, regarding them all. Weapons were drawn and a solemn focus came over the unit. "Hiss, Lena, Bayon and I will go down to the Sub," he said. "Rosalie, Talon, Mal and Rage, you clean the second level. Lian and Keira check the other floors. Take out as many staff as you can, then we're going out the front door with the captives. Alisa, Jessa, Pride and Striker will be waiting with the vans. Backup cars are parked around the building, keys inside. Use them only if you can't get out, can't get to the vans." He looked at each one of them. "Are we clear?"

Everyone nodded.

"Be careful. I want no accidents. We are all going home alive."

No one nodded or confirmed this. They didn't have to.

Parish tossed them a dark, menacing grin. "Let's go hunting," he said before he disappeared into the stairwell.

Focused tension clung to them as they descended. Every eye looking out for movement. Every ear listening for footfall. With each level they reached, a pack broke off and, with a silent nod of understanding, went to work. Until finally, Hiss, Parish, Lena and Bayon were at ground level.

The Sub.

Surprisingly, being back inside the lab didn't fill Hiss with fear or anxiety. Just purpose. After performing a quick audio scan of the long, cold, dark room, they moved in. The familiar scents rushed Hiss's nostrils. "Blade?" he whispered into the dark.

"Hiss?" the male called out.

"Yeah."

All around the room, shifters stirred in their cages. Without being able to see all that well, Hiss could only guess they were at the doors of their cages, waiting for the sign to emerge.

"I knew we could trust you," Blade said when Hiss and Parish reached him. Lena and Bayon were on the opposite side, gathering the shifters together.

"A promise is a promise," Hiss told him.

The male clapped his shoulder. "We've been waiting. I almost lost those keys to Peter. Had to cut a hole in my mattress."

A sudden smattering of gunfire erupted on the floor above.

"Get down!" Parish commanded, brandishing his weapon and heading for the stairwell.

Everyone except the Hunters did as they were instructed. For several seconds, Parish listened at the door. Waited. When there was no second round of gunfire, he turned back.

"We've got to get out of here now." He signaled to Hiss and the others to bring the shifters to him. "I know all of you are pumas, and you'll want to fight. But I also know you've been through it, and might not have your normal strength. Whatever you can do is appreciated. We're glad to have more fighters beside us."

A hum of understanding and agreement went through the group of males and females. And as they made their way up the stairs to the first floor and the lobby and the waiting vans just outside, a solid readiness blanketed them too.

That is, until they pulled back the last locked door and came face to face with a small militia of armed guards. For several seconds, no one moved. The shifters watched the guards, and vice versa. Until Hiss saw that one of them had Rosalie in a headlock, a Glock to her temple.

Without Parish's consent, he sprang forward, taking out one guard with his fists and another with the butt of his gun. He had to get to Rosalie. She, of all of them, needed to live through this raid. She'd already sacrificed enough to their enemies' cause. Behind him he heard Parish give the signal and the Hunters and escaping Pantera converged on the guards. Shots peppered the air, along with the sounds of bones cracking and blood spattering and Pantera snarling.

Spotting Hiss's approach, the guard who had Rosalie starting dragging her backward, toward the lobby. Hiss followed. *Not happening, asshole. She's coming home with me.*

"Back off, animal," the guard warned him, pressing the gun harder against Rosalie's temple. "Or do you want her brains splattered all over you?"

Rosalie's eyes were pinned on Hiss. And in that moment, it was like the old days. When Hunters communicated through sight, both in their male and female forms, and as cats. She was telling him not to back off. To keep coming, and when she signaled—

There it was! As Hiss rushed the male, Rosalie propelled her body forward, then slammed her elbow back into his stomach. The guard's gun discharged, sending a bullet into the ceiling.

"Drop it," Hiss growled, taking him to the ground.

"Fuck you, animal," the guard spat back, jerking his hand up, trying to aim the gun at Hiss's head.

Hiss closed his hand around the man's fist, and in under five seconds, he had the gun in his possession and had tossed it to Rosalie. Just as a fist slammed into his face, he heard a shot. The guard beneath him went limp.

"There was a breeze on that bullet," he said dryly

to Rosalie as he climbed to his feet.

For the first time, she faced him. Really looked at him. And as a battle raged around them, as the lab's unwilling subjects started to spill out into the lobby and head for the doors, she continued to stare.

"I'm so sorry, Rosa," he said. "I have nothing else but that to give you. I know it's not much. Not enough."

"It's something," she said finally.

He nodded, the pain in his body a mere pinch compared to the pain in his heart—or her eyes. In seeking vengeance for his family, he'd broken someone else's, and he would spend his life making up for it.

"Let's go back in," she said.

"No, I'll go," he told her. "You take the ones we rescued."

"You sure?"

He nodded. "I'll help Parish."

"See you back at the van," she said before taking off with the group of humans.

Heading in the opposite direction, Hiss found Parish and Bayon and Lena among the bodies of the guards. They were herding Pantera, humans and children toward the door.

"Where's Hakan?" Hiss demanded. He hadn't seen the male pass by when he was with Rosalie.

"He was just here," Bayon said. "But he spotted a guard making for the stairwell. Went after him."

"I'm going to check it out. See if he needs backup."

Parish nodded. "We need to get these people out

168

of here before the human police arrive. Use one of the cars, if you have to. We'll meet you back home?"

It was a split second only between them. A question to be answered. A question of trust. Maybe a question for possible forgiveness as well.

Are you coming back? Are you coming home?

Hiss nodded, then took off. Covered in blood and bruises, he hit the stairwell. Gun drawn, he listened for sounds. Nothing. It felt like how night always felt in the Sub. *Hakan, where the hell are you?* Maybe the Hunter had followed the guard all the way up to the roof.

He took the steps two at a time until he reached the door. He opened it gingerly in case something was on the other side. But all he found was pre-dawn sky, a cloud-covered moon, an empty roof.

Cold air rushed over his hot, sweaty, pained skin. He stalked across the tiles to the parapet and looked out. The vans were moving now. Each going in a different direction. He'd have to grab a car. He heard the sirens wailing. In minutes, cops would be all over this place. Hakan must've gotten out.

"You are a very good fighter, Hiss."

The voice stopped him. Cold. Stunned. He whirled around. Not ten feet away a woman stood, bracketed by two guards. They looked fresh, as if they hadn't been in the battle. Hiss's eyes moved over her. Tall, slender, with dark hair pulled up in a knot atop her head.

"I didn't imagine it," he called out.

His mother's green eyes warmed in the hazy moonlight. "No, my son."

Those two words wrapped around and squeezed. Goddess, how many times had he wished to hear his mother's voice? He started toward her, was about to urge her to take his hand, to come with him—to escape—when he stopped. When he realized...

"You're not captive here, are you?"

She shook her head.

His gut seized.

"I'm a guest," she said. "Of Christopher's."

Hiss knew that name. Stanton Locke's boss. The big boss. The benefactor. The one who ran this freak show.

"You're a guest of the monster who runs this place?" he called. What the hell was happening?

"Don't call him that!"

He stared at her.

"He's your father, Hiss." Her face warmed. "Don't you want to know him?"

Cold sickness assaulted him. What was she saying? Father? That couldn't be true. That would mean he was a hybrid. No.

No. He was full-blooded Pantera.

"It's true," she told him. "I wanted so badly to have a child, and well, your father and I... When I met Christopher it was only to become pregnant. To find a way to become pregnant. He is a genius in the field of medical research, and has unlimited resources. I was going to be inseminated, you see, then return to the Wildlands. But once we were together..." Her face lit up. Actually lit up with happiness. "I couldn't walk away from him then and I can't walk away from him now."

Pure unadulterated ire ripped into Hiss, killing the cold sickness. She was serious in her madness. "The asshole who had my blood drained? Who kept human and Pantera prisoners? Who tortured and experimented and brought pain to god knows how many living creatures?" The sirens were drawing closer. And yet she wasn't moving. Why wasn't she running? Why wasn't she afraid? "That is my biological father."

"He needs it to live," she explained, as if what she was saying was sane and moralistically okay. "He can't survive without it. Now that he doesn't have your sister..."

"Reny," he breathed. Goddess, could he ever tell her this truth? He could barely stomach it himself.

"I regret using Reny. But Christopher was so ill. He needed blood, and mine was too strong, too powerful."

Hiss stared at the vile creature before him. The creature he'd built up to be a virtual saint in his mind.

"I can't believe I mourned you. And all this time you were fucking around with a sociopath, giving no thought to your true family."

Her face fell.

"The elders," he ground out. "They told me you and Dad and Reny died in a fire."

"Your Pantera father did," she said. "The elders must've believed that we all perished that way. Or chose to ignore the possibility that we hadn't." She took a step forward. "Hiss don't go."

For one tiny, ridiculous second he believed she meant that in the way a true mother would've meant it. But as the police cars screeched to a stop at the curb down below, and a helicopter made its way toward the roof, he realized she was scared for Christopher. The man's blood donor was running—and his many others had already escaped. How was he to stay alive?

"Go fuck yourself," he ground out, then turned and leapt from the building to the roof next door, then to the roof of the Chauncey.

He never looked back until he was down the stairs and out on the streets. He'd never look back again. It was all forward. The future, and hope for forgiveness.

Coming out of the alley behind the hotel, he jerked to a stop when a car pulled up in front of him. The window went down and Hakan gave him a wry smile.

"Funny meeting you here, Hunter," he said dryly.

Hiss felt his guts uncurl a bit. "Damn, brother, I looked everywhere for you."

"Well, you found me. Or I found you." He knocked his head in the direction of the passenger side. "Need a ride?"

Hiss slipped into the car, and the moment he slammed the door shut, the Hunter took off into the night. He didn't say much until they were on the road toward home.

"You feel like talking?" Hakan asked.

"Ran into my mother. On the roof of the lab."

Hakan's head came around so fast he nearly hit another car. "What? I thought she was dead."

"So did I. Turns out she's not only alive, but Christopher's mate." He inhaled sharply. "She was serving up her children's blood to that…" He couldn't even finish.

"Fuck, I'm sorry," Hakan said, dropping a hand on Hiss's shoulder.

"So am I," Hiss returned, staring out the window at the coming dawn. "For being such a blind fool for so goddamned long. That ends today."

***

Gia's puma had found something it loved in the Wildlands: the bayou. The warm water mixed with the cool morning air made the cat feel at peace. And after last night, and the many months of cage-dwelling, she craved peace. She didn't think the water where she was swimming now was the same water that Hiss had told her of. She hadn't seen any of those lilies, and there had been no feeling of control over her cat.

Hiss.

She tried not to allow her mind to go there. Think of him. Wonder about his safety. She was too pissed.

Her ears pricked up, catching the sound of something coming toward the bayou. She didn't think it was the guards. They hadn't been around since last night. But maybe it was Hiss. Maybe he was back.

Her cat stalked out of the bayou, stood on the shore and shook. But the sound that met her ears next was a shriek. A woman's shriek. She sniffed the air just as a human woman emerged. She was very pretty, with long, black curls and big brown eyes. She was wiping water from her face and sort of laughing.

"That's some spray," she said. "You could beat Keira's record. And not even Parish can do that."

Gia shifted into her female form and grabbed the towel she'd left on the tree branch. Wrapping it around herself, she stepped forward. "Who are you?" she asked.

"Oh, sorry," the woman apologized, shaking her head. "I'm Ashe. Raphael is my mate."

"But…you're human," she stuttered.

Ashe grinned. "I am. And we have a daughter. Soyala."

Gia was fascinated. "Is that common here? Human/puma matings?"

"Becoming more so," Ashe told her. "I'm afraid the human world is encroaching on us."

"I pray that doesn't happen in my Wetlands." Then realizing what she'd said, Gia backed up a little. "I didn't mean the matings. Just the human world as a whole. It's how I was taken and brought to the lab. Dealing with humans."

Ashe's face grew sympathetic. "I'm so sorry about what you've had to go through. I'm glad you're here. We want you to feel at home. Raphael and I."

"Thank you."

"And Hiss wanted to make sure—"

"Hiss asked you to check on me, didn't he?" Gia interrupted. Unbelievable. "He has a conversation with you, but writes me a note."

"He actually asked Raphael, but I get it." Ashe grimaced. "Sorry."

"Don't be. I appreciate you coming here."

"Men are weird and great and a total pain the ass sometimes." Ashe gestured to the water. "But it looks like you're enjoying your time without him."

"I'm a water Hunter back home. For my sect. My cat is drawn to it."

"Right." Ashe was staring at her.

"What?"

174

"Well...aren't you curious? About where he is? What he's doing? Why he left in the middle of the night?" She shrugged. "I can't get a thing out of Raph, and he's usually so forthcoming. Bastard."

Gia wasn't always taken with humans, especially after what had been done to her, but she couldn't help liking this one. She was incredible charming. "I know where Hiss is."

"You do?"

She nodded. "And I know what he's doing. He's with the Hunters, in Baton Rogue, trying to get the lab cleared out, the shifters and children out." She exhaled heavily, refusing to think he was anything but okay. It wasn't her way to worry and pine and hope. "I'm not surprised by his desire to go with them. We all have to do what we have to do."

Ashe regarded her. "And what are you going to do?"

"Go home," Gia said, her chest tightening a little. "I spoke with my family this morning. They were so happy, so emotional, so relieved. They'd feared the worst. I didn't give them a ton of details. I thought that would be better to do in person. But they begged me to come home."

"Of course they did," Ashe said.

"I really like your Wildlands. It's a wonderful place. For many reasons." She smiled softly, knowingly. "But nothing compares to my home. To my Wetlands."

"I understand," Ashe said. "To be honest, there's not all that much out in the human world for me. But I still feel the connection. The pull. I still wonder about family I don't know."

175

"You should pursue that," Gia told her. "Knowledge, information, those are good things. Whether you want to act on them or not."

"You're very…decided, you know that?"

Gia laughed. "I think the word you're looking for is opinionated."

Ashe shrugged. "Maybe. Whatever it is, whatever it's called, it's refreshing. Can I sit with you awhile? Raphael is with Soyala this morning at Headquarters. It'd be nice to have some big girl time."

"Be my guest. Of course," she amended on a laugh, "I'm kind of your guest, but…"

Ashe dissolved into laughter. "The only thing we're missing right now is cocktails."

"I make a mean margarita," Gia told her.

Slamming her hands together, prayer-style, Ashe cried, "Don't go!"

Laughter bubbled within Gia again. "In the absence of tequila, we have the magic of the bayou. You like to swim?"

"Not sure how that dark, creature-infested water is going to give me a buzz, but okay. I'm more of a swimming pool chick myself."

"You'll love it," Gia told her with a wicked grin.

"I don't have a suit."

Gia dropped her towel. "Neither do I."

At first, Ashe looked a little startled. Then she laughed. "Oh, god. Okay." She started to strip. "But if one of the Hunters or Suits or god forbid, Geeks sees me naked, I'm blaming you."

"Good thing I won't be around for long," Gia called merrily over her shoulder as she headed for the water.

CHAPTER 9

The morning sun was high in the cloudless blue sky as Hiss left Suit Headquarters and headed for the cottage. For Gia. He'd been back in the Wildlands only short time, meeting with Raphael and Parish, debriefing the mission and where they all went from here.

A new day had dawned in so many ways. Both in and out of the Wildlands. Headquarters was now packed to the gills with captives from the lab—Pantera, human and hybrid. And each was welcome to decide where they wanted to be. The Pantera would help regardless.

For Hiss, the new day brought an end to the charges he faced. After Rosalie had gone to Raphael and told him how Hiss had saved her life, and the lives of so many, the decision to keep him captive was revoked. There was no doubt that Hiss was relieved, even grateful for this. But all that had happened, from years previous to just a few hours ago on the roof of that lab, still weighed heavily on him. He felt like his Pantera brothers and sisters would forgive him in time—some already had—but there would always be a cloud over his sun here.

Reny would need to hear the truth from him. He couldn't imagine how she would take the news of their mother's treachery. But right now, he had to see Gia. Had to hold her. Look in her eyes and know he was home.

He spotted the cottage in the distance, smelled the warm earthy scent of the bayou, and his insides liquefied. Goddess, he needed her. Like air to the lungs.

As he drew closer, her scent filled his nostrils. What was she doing? he wondered. What had she been doing? Raphael had told him that Ashe had visited her early this morning. It was all he'd told Hiss, which had been slightly odd. As if the male was holding something back.

The house was quiet when he entered.

"Gia?" he called. "*Ma chère?*"

When there was no response, he headed for the bedroom. Where her scent was the strongest. The bed was still unmade, white sheets askew, reminding him of what they'd shared last night. But there was no Gia.

His eyes caught on the small garbage basket beside the bed. At the bottom was a crumpled piece of paper. His gut tightened and a strain of fear rippled through him. His note? He reached in and took out the paper.

Dammit, she'd been angry. What had Raphael been holding back? What had Ashe told him? Maybe Gia had confided her ire in the human woman. Told her she no longer cared for him.

Fuck, he was spinning.

On a growl of impatience, he left the bedroom

178

and searched every other room before heading back outside.

Had Gia been so angry with him for leaving without telling her that she didn't want to be with him anymore? Was that possible? He dropped onto one of the porch steps and scrubbed a hand over his face. He was an idiot. An asshole. How could he let something like this happen? She'd asked for honesty from him. That's all she'd wanted. Had she interpreted leaving without telling her as dishonesty?

Hiss sat on that step for an hour, waiting, mentally beating the shit out of himself. This was it. She wasn't coming back. No doubt she was on her way home, to the Wetlands. And he was getting what he deserved. The law of nature. He had taken and hurt so many. Now it was his turn.

A wave of such terrible pain blanketed him. He'd found forgiveness and redemption in the Pantera. He was free. And yet he wished to be back in the lab, in a cage, beside her. The knife he still had strapped to his ankle hummed. He slipped it out and held it. Stared at it.

"What the hell do you think you're doing?"

The breath left his lungs as his head came up. Not five feet away stood the female he'd just been grieving. His eyes skimmed over her, from long, bare legs to cut-off jean shorts and a blue tank top. She looked as edible as always. Her blond hair was piled on top of her head, a few strays bracketing her beautiful face. How had he not heard her? How had he not scented her? The blade in his hand felt cold and he thrust it aside. He wanted warm. He wanted heat.

I want my mate.

"Gia?" He couldn't believe it. Couldn't believe his insane mind, and all it had conjured in the past hour. "Oh, fuck, *ma chère*. You're here. You're still here."

She stared at him like he was crazy. She wasn't wrong. He was mad. For her. For their life together. He didn't want to live it without her.

"Of course I'm here," she said. "Look." She held up the basket in her hands. Inside were about twenty Dyesse lilies. "I've been searching everywhere for these. For you. For when you returned." Her gaze searched his. "Where else would I be, Hiss?"

He was truly a male gone mad. And undeserving…so undeserving…

"You thought I'd left you, did you?" she asked. "Over that?" she pointed at the note.

Hiss hadn't even realized he'd brought it out here, much less that he'd been holding it. He nodded, cursed and tossed that aside too.

She walked up to him, placed the basket beside him and crawled into his arms. Her eyes found his, and she leaned in and kissed him on the mouth. "In case you've forgotten, I mated you."

"I haven't forgotten," he uttered, his body reacting instantly to her closeness.

"Where you go, I go," she said then kissed him again. "If that's here or the Wetlands. Even if I'm pissed. Even if I want to slug you for not waking me up and telling me where you're going."

His hands went around her, crushed her to him. He growled. "Goddess, I love you, female."

"And I love you," she returned. "But don't do that again, okay?"

180

"I promise." He couldn't believe this was happening. Her with him. Always. Forever. Wildlands, or maybe the Wetlands. He liked that idea. A new adventure. Starting fresh.

He stood up then, taking her and the basket of lilies with him. She wrapped her legs around his waist and held on tight as he carried her inside. He needed her. More than air this time. It was something far more special, more primitive…

Something only claimed lovers understood.

Once inside the bedroom, he set her down gently and started removing her clothes, then his own.

"So have you decided to mate me, then?" she asked, completely comfortable in her skin. Her luscious, highly addictive skin.

Totally naked now, Hiss grabbed the basket of flowers and started tossing the blooms onto the bed. He was going to take her surrounded by Dyesse lilies. "Oh, that's already a done deal, *ma chère*."

"I don't think so," she said with a wicked thread to her voice.

He tossed the basket aside and stalked toward her. "What do you mean, Gia?" he growled. "Make no mistake, you are mine."

"Of course I am." Her brown eyes flashed. "But in my sect, we make it official in a very special way."

He stopped in front of her. "I like the sound of that."

"Good." Before he could say another word, she shifted into her cat—a medium-sized gray puma with very mischievous eyes.

For a couple of seconds the puma pawed the

ground. Then it came at him, knocking him onto the bed. Snarling, it jumped up beside him and started nuzzling his neck. Hiss had no idea what kind of ritual they were getting into until the cat bit down on his hand.

A curse fell from his lips as blood bubbled up from the two small holes.

Suddenly, the cat shook and shimmered, and in front of him, gloriously naked, blond hair licking the tips of her hard nipples, was his mate. She took his hand and lapped at the blood.

Hiss's cock went steel-hard.

"Now take me, male," she commanded, crawling onto the bed on all fours. "Only when your body is in mine will I truly belong to you."

The cat inside of Hiss roared, and he was on her in an instant.

"Mine," he gritted out, his cock pressed against the entrance to her sex.

"Almost," she teased, circling her hips.

With one hard thrust, Hiss was inside her.

Warm.

Wet.

Heaven.

And Gia, his love, his life and his mate, softly snarled back, "Yours."

ABOUT THE AUTHORS

Alexandra Ivy is a *New York Times* and *USA Today* bestselling author of the Guardians of Eternity series, as well as the Immortal Rogues. After majoring in theatre she decided she prefers to bring her characters to life on paper rather than stage. She lives in Missouri with her family. Visit her website at alexandraivy.com.

New York Times and USA Today Bestselling Author, **Laura Wright** is passionate about romantic fiction. Though she has spent most of her life immersed in acting, singing and competitive ballroom dancing, when she found the world of writing and books and endless cups of coffee she knew she was home. Laura is the author of the bestselling Mark of the Vampire series and the USA Today bestselling series, Bayou Heat, which she co-authors with Alexandra Ivy.

Laura lives in Los Angeles with her husband, two young children and three loveable dogs.

CPSIA information can be obtained
at www.ICGtesting.com
Printed in the USA
BVOW03s0227070817
491341BV00001B/1/P